*The Engleburt Stories*

*North to the Tropics*

# The Engleburt Stories

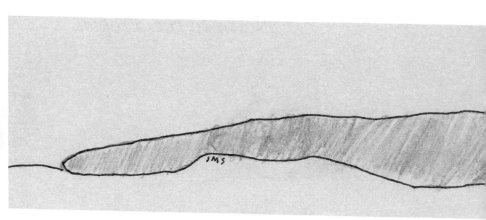

*PAJ Publications*
*New York*

# North to the Tropics

by

## Samuel MacIntosh-Schechner
### and
### Richard Schechner

*Illustrations by Samuel MacIntosh-Schechner*

*To Lilah Schechner*
*with whom these stories were first shared*

© 1987 Copyright by PAJ Publications

First Edition

**Library of Congress Cataloging in Publication Data**
The Engleburt Stories: North to the Tropics
Library of Congress Catalog Card No.: 87-81203
ISBN: 1-55554-024-4

Printed in the United States of America

Publication of this book has been made possible in part by grants received from the National Endowment for the Arts, Washington, D.C., a federal agency, and the New York State Council on the Arts.

# The Engleburt Stories

# North to the Tropics

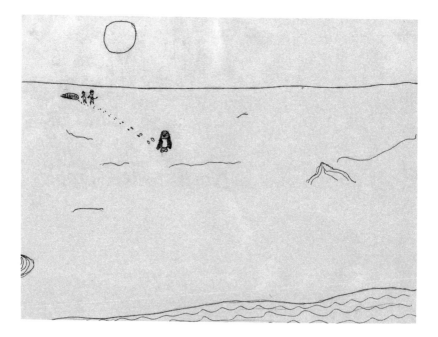

# The Ice Pit

 ENGLEBURT is an Adélie penguin, the kind with orange feet. He used to live in Antarctica—which was named after a crusty old penguin named Arctica whom everybody called ''aunt.'' She was an old, difficult penguin—always screaming and flapping her wings. But everyone loved her. When she died—actually she was eaten by a huge white adventuresome polar bear who was the first of his species to explore the south pole—all the penguins gathered together and named their continent after old aunt Arctica.

One thing about Antarctica, it is very very cold. Not only is there snow all year round, but there is a terrible and brutal wind that chills even penguins through their feathers. Actually, during the warmest months of the summer—which down there in the southmost part of the world comes in December and January—there are places that fill with grass and carpets of yellow dandelions. These are little hollows sheltered from the wind, facing north looking into the sun.

Engleburt knew he was a penguin but thought he should have been born a parrot or a bird of paradise or a peacock—some marvelous tropical feathered flying thing. He longed for palm trees, pineapples, plums, and purple sunsets. He wanted to bathe his orange toes in luke warm oceans. So Engleburt decided to set out for the tropics.

He didn't know where he was heading except north. He didn't know where his travels would take him except past the equator.

So early one bright December morning Engleburt began to trudge north, following the sun. He saw clear ice ahead. And then he walked on to where the sun's warmth made the ice mushy. Two minutes later he stepped on some crunchy ice, and whoops! it gave way and Engleburt plunged into a great blue ice chamber.

Engleburt was a bird but he couldn't fly. Penguins can't fly. They are fabulous swimmers who fly underwater, but that couldn't help Engleburt now. He said to himself, "How am I going to get out of here?" He looked at the walls of shiny, slippery ice. He thought that soon warm December would become January and January would become cool February and then it would get colder and darker and colder still and he would freeze to death—if he didn't starve to death first.

When he had all but given up hope, he heard footsteps overhead. "Who is that?" he thought, excited and frightened all together. Because no people live in Antarctica—there are no Eskimos there. But no matter who—or what—was above him, Engleburt had no choice but to get their attention. He started squeaking—that's what penguins do, you know—and flapping his wings as if he could suddenly invent flying. He squeaked louder and louder—he wanted to sound like a whole flock of penguins. And sure enough, Engleburt soon saw a human face looking over the rim of his icy prison.

"Hey, John" a woman shouted, "come look what I found! A penguin's trapped down there."

Two human faces were peering down at Engleburt who flapped and squeaked even more. Engleburt tried to talk to the people. If they could've understood him, this is what they would've heard: "Please help me! I fell in here! Get me out! All I want to do is to find a tropical island!" And they would have heard him ask: "Who are you? What are you doing here? Don't shoot me!

Don't eat me! Help me, please help me!''

Engleburt was glad but he was also frightened because he knew that some humans were cruel. Some people shoot penguins and seals and whales and bears. He didn't want to be shot. But these humans—Veeny and her friend John—were scientists, and they wanted only to help. John was a geologist from America and Veeny was a zoologist from India. John had never been to Antarctica before but Veeny had been there twice. Her brother, Suresh, was also a zoologist—and she had come south with him.

Veeny was very interested in Engleburt. As John tied a rope to an ice pick that he planted firmly in the solid ice, Veeny said: ''I wonder how that bird got there? Penguins are very social—but this fellow is alone.'' It really was a mystery. When Veeny and John were sure the rope was very very secure, they tied the loose end around Veeny and John lowered her down. She talked calmly to Engleburt. ''Don't be frightened, come here, come here.'' And she opened her arms. But she didn't have to worry. Engleburt wanted very much to get out of that deep cold ice pit. As soon as Veeny was within a few feet of him, Engleburt flapped his wings with excitement and thanks—he jumped into her arms with such force that he knocked her down.

''Hey,'' Veeny cried, ''watch out or you'll start an avalanche in here and neither of us will get out—ever.''

As soon as Engleburt calmed down—Veeny hummed a nice soothing melody into his feathers where she knew his ears were—John began hauling the rope up. Veeny carefully found toe holds in the wall of ice—and before too long she and Engleburt were up and free.

Immediately, without even squeaking ''thank you,'' Engleburt jumped out of Veeny's arms and ran north.

''What a strange penguin,'' Veeny said. ''I've never seen anything like him before.'' Soon the black and white bird had disappeared in the immense snowfield.

# The Southern Ocean

ENGLEBURT knew he had to travel fast—January was nearly over and winter would soon blow across Antarctica, freezing even the seas and making any northward journey impossible. Soon he reached the coast of Antarctica. He looked out at the gray ocean teeming with whales and seals and sea lions and walruses. All these great mammals had come south for the rich plankton of the summer sea.

Without a moment's hesitation or regret, Engleburt jumped into the sea and ducked under the water—where penguins can fly in the deep as swiftly and gracefully as eagles in the air.

A great sense of joy overwhelmed him because he knew he was on his way north—at last!

Engleburt started swimming with such speed that he bumped into a blue whale.

A blue whale is immense—it is the biggest animal ever to have lived on the planet earth. And this blue whale was almost 100 feet long.

That's much bigger than a big bus.

But despite his great size, the blue whale was very gentle—and he and Engleburt soon became friends.

Blue whales eat plankton only. Plankton consists of drifting small organisms—little plants and animals—that the great blue whale eats in giant strainerfuls as he swims through the Antarctic seas.

Whales strain the plankton through a big sieve made of soft bone—which is called baleen. This whalebone is very soft, as soft as silk, and in it the giant whale collects the thousands of tiny plants and animals it feeds its great hulk on.

The whale introduced himself. "My name's Buster," he squeaked to Engleburt—because whales like penguins talk by squeaking. That's why Engleburt and Buster could talk to each other.

"I'm going north," Engleburt said, "and I want you to come with me."

"Sure, I'd be glad to. I need to go north too—it gets too cold around here in the winter."

"Where are you heading?" asked Engleburt.

"Oh, up past the Cape and down the middle of the Atlantic and then across the Bahamas."

Engleburt didn't know what or where any of these places were. But he didn't want to appear dumb to his new friend so he just said, "That sounds terrific. I'll go with you." After they had been swimming for a few hours—Buster just plunging along making great waves and spewing fountains of water and air up through his blow hole, Engleburt diving and surfacing, spinning and flipping upside down in the increasingly warm water—Engleburt got up enough courage to ask:

"Hey, are the Bahamas relatives of yours, or what?" Engleburt thought Bahamas meant "behemoth," which is another word for whale.

Buster rolled with laughter. He flapped his great fluke with outrageous hilarity. He made tidal waves and almost shipwrecked three Argentine fishing boats. "Relatives! No, my dear little penguin, the Bahamas are the most beautiful, peaceful, warm tropical islands you can imagine."

"Oh, take me there," cried Engleburt. "That's where I want to live."

So they kept swimming north.

They went past South Sandwich Island and then past South Georgia Island. Just north of South Georgia some Portuguese fishermen laughed at the sight of a huge blue whale with a tiny black and white penguin riding on his back. Because that's exactly what happened.

When Engleburt got tired Buster said, "Hop on my back for a free ride!"

At first Engleburt was scared. "What if I fall off? What if you roll over and pin me underneath you?" Buster said, "I thought penguins were the world's best swimming birds."

"Oh, yes," cried Engleburt, "that's true. But I don't have any practice in bareback whale riding."

Buster smiled with his ten-thousand plankton-straining hairs that blue whales have instead of teeth. "Don't worry," he said, "I'll be very careful."

And he was.

# Attacked By Sharks

SO THEY kept swimming north through warmer seas and thunderstorms and flocks of seagulls. They passed a school of porpoises. "Hey," cried Buster, "Over here! Hi!" But the dolphins—another name for porpoises—were so busy chattering and playing and diving that they didn't even bother to answer Buster. "Those are my cousins," Buster said. "But sometimes those porpoises can be very snobby." He and Engleburt swam on.

Soon they were in the quiet waters midway between Africa and South America near the tiny island of St. Helena. But the calm waters were deceptive. Riding on Buster's back Engleburt saw to the left what looked like a tiny shark face with red eyes.

"What's going on here," Engleburt said. "Who is this little fish? And why are its eyes so red?" Buster, big as he was, didn't want to have anything to do with sharks.

"Come on," he said to his feathered friend, "don't bother with sharks—even small ones. They have lots of teeth, you know. They're born with dozens of little razor-sharp teeth that can cut you to shreds before you know it."

"Oh, come on," said Engleburt, "that's just a little baby and you're the biggest fish in the world."

Buster answered, "I'm not a fish, I'm a mammal. And I bet when you were a little baby, a shrimp came up to you and said, 'Oh, look at that cute little baby penguin.' But when that unsuspecting shrimp got close enough you gulped him up. I'm not going near any shark—where there's one shark there are ten sharks and where there are ten sharks there are a hundred."

But then both Buster and Engleburt heard the baby shark cry out.

"Oh, oh, where is my mommy?!" And the little shark swam right for Engleburt.

"Have you seen my mommy?" asked the baby shark in the smallest, squeakiest, most pitiable shark voice you have ever heard. Engleburt spread his wings and invited the baby shark to rest amid his warm feathers.

Without a second's hesitation the shark swam in and snuggled her face under Engleburt's wingpit.

Buster was not happy with the arrangement at all. "You'll be sorry," he warned, "and so will I."

But Engleburt liked his adopted shark baby. He cooed and cuddled and squeaked to it. He made big eyes at it. He stroked it with his wings and fed it little fish. And so on they swam, this strange family of whale, penguin, and shark.

But then suddenly in the middle of the great gray ocean Buster caught sight of a silvery triangle moving zigzag in the calm waters. "Uh-oh," Buster grunted. And the baby shark saw the triangle too and cried out with all her strength, "Mommyyy!!"

At once, the silvery triangle made a beeline for Engleburt. This mommy shark was all teeth. She was a Great White shark, and she was very mad.

"You let go of my baby!" she cried out in shark language.

All Engleburt could hear was a roar and all he could see was five rows of white, sharp, dangerous teeth.

"Hey," Engleburt squeaked at the top of his lungs, "I was just being nice to this lost baby!"

"Lost baby!" cried the mother shark, "that's my baby—and now I'm going to feed it chopped penguin for supper!"

"Hold on," said Buster in his deepest, whalest, strongest voice.

But the mother shark angrily shouted, "You stay out of this, you plankton-eating big blob of blubber!" But then a small small voice piped up.

"Don't get mad at my friends, mommy."

It was the little baby Great White shark. She knew the truth. And she had the courage to say it out loud. "This penguin saw me crying and held me and fed me and made me feel better when I was lost. And this big whale let me take a nap on one of his soft blue flukes. It was so warm."

The mother shark calmed down a little.

"The name's Gertrude," she said. "And I'm sorry to have lost my temper—I have a very short one." Then she gave a great big shark laugh, flashing all of her rows of teeth, hundreds of gleaming white shining triangles of sharpness.

"But I was so worried about my little Angelina."

Engleburt replied, "Oh, it's ok, we understand how worried a parent can be. But Angelina is fine now."

The little shark swam over to her mommy. She nestled in a special spot right next to her mommy's left gill slits.

Then Buster said, "Well, it's time we were on our way. We're going to the Bahamas."

Angelina looked longingly at her mother. But Gertrude shook her big white head, squinting a little with her round shark's eyes.

"No, my baby, we can't go in that direction. We have to meet a vast school of Great Whites up near the Azores."

"Where's that?" Engleburt asked.

"On the other side of the Atlantic Ocean," Gertrude replied. Then she looked a little troubled—a small furrow appearing over her right eye. "And anyway, to tell the truth, I don't think you would be happy there. I know how nice you've been to Angelina, but my shark relations won't know. They have a special taste for fowl." And when Gertrude laughed again Engleburt felt a shiver go up his spine.

"You do have sharp, sharp teeth," he said. "And so many of

them."

"You must spend hours at the dentist!" Buster said, winking at Engleburt.

Gertrude laughed again.

"Actually, there's a special coral reef near Australia that I just love to rub my teeth against. That's how I keep them clean." Then she swam very close to Engleburt. "Go on," she said, "put your head in, take a look." Engleburt wanted to have nothing to do with this inspection.

"I know they're clean, I don't have to look."

"Oh, go ahead," Angelina said, "Mommy won't bite your head off."

"She said she likes fowl," Engleburt answered.

Gertrude opened her mouth so wide Engleburt could see right down into her great green stomach. Angelina swam over to Engleburt. "I'll swim with you," she said reassuringly.

After a moment's hesitation, Engleburt took the plunge. He swam right into Gertrude's mouth. It was like being inside a vast snowy mountain range with peak after peak of snow-capped mountains. He whistled to keep up his bravery. Outside Buster watched very closely, on the alert to save his friend if anything dangerous should happen.

But nothing did.

Gertrude was actually a very kind and gentle shark. And soon Engleburt and Angelina were swimming among the rows of teeth, laughing and gurgling. Finally, Gertrude shook her head, signaling that she had had enough. Engleburt and Angelina exited.

"We really must be on our way," Gertrude said. "Come, Angy."

The little shark got in position underneath her mother. And with a swift stroke of her powerful tail the Great White shark surged off into the blue Atlantic.

Buster and Engleburt lazily swam off in a northwesterly direction. They swam for a long time, not saying anything. They were at peace with the world and with each other. The water was warm, the sea calm. Above them fleecy white clouds smiled. The air smelled sweet and clean.

They had no idea they were swimming straight into the territory of the Giant Ones.

# The Giant Ones

 AFTER TWO days of the calmest water imaginable the ocean suddenly turned choppy. It was very strange because there was no wind, and the sky remained peaceful, except for six looming shadows near the western horizon. What could be causing the sudden roughness in the sea?

Just as the sun was setting on that second day they heard what sounded like humming. At first, neither Engleburt nor Buster dared say anything—each thought maybe he was hearing imaginary sounds.

But then Engleburt paddled up to Buster's right exterior ear drum—whales don't have ears shaped like we do—and said quietly, "Do you hear something?"

"A humming?" Buster asked tentatively.

"In a consistent tone?" Engleburt said with growing excitement.

"Coming from over there?" Buster waved his fluke toward the west.

"Right!"

They swam a while and listened.

"What do you think it is?" Engleburt asked.

"Don't know," said Buster. "Should we swim over towards it

and find out what it is?''

''Let's wait till morning,'' Engleburt answered. ''I'm a little scared.''

Then, all of a sudden, like a thunderclap, they heard a roar of a song! Both Engleburt and Buster stopped dead in the water. Engleburt swept back his feathers so he could hear better. And dimly in the early evening darkness he saw six great big shapes about ten miles away to the northwest. He was sure the singing was coming from that direction. And, what was worse, he was sure the six great big shapes were moving toward him.

Sure enough, they were. And soon enough Buster and Engleburt could make out clearly what the big shapes were singing. This was their song:

> We are the Giant Ones
> The Giant Ones, the Giant Ones!
> We are the Giant Ones
> We're so tall
> You can never tell
> Where we begin or end!!
> BEEEEEEP!!!

The Giant Ones kept singing this song over and over and over. Buster and Engleburt thought maybe these six Giant Ones were having some kind of a party. But at least they stopped advancing.

''They probably don't know we're here,'' Engleburt said.

And even the giant blue whale was a little scared.

Buster said, ''Maybe we should try to sleep. We'll need all our energy tomorrow.''

''Ok,'' replied Engleburt. And he snuggled up so very close to Buster. He pressed himself into Buster's side—almost disappearing in Buster's rolls of blue blubber. And as he dozed off he could still hear in the distance the great rolling rollicking singing of the Giant Ones:

> We're so tall
> You can never tell

Where we begin or end!!
BEEEEEEP!!!

# Bad Dreams, Good Dreams

BUSTER HAD this terrible dream that night. He dreamt that he was in the ocean deep down at the bottom of the sea. And suddenly a big gust of water slammed against his back. He tried to swim away but he got smooshed by the leg of a Giant One.

Engleburt, on the other hand, had this dream. He climbed up a Giant One's leg, passed the Giant's waist-line to her shoulder—for this Giant One was definitely a she—and snuggled sleepily in her warm salty-smelling hair. He made friends with her. Her name was Margaret. He dreamt that he said goodbye to Buster and went away with Margaret. Before he could discover where he and Margaret went, he woke up.

He woke up just in time to see Buster rolling over and screaming the most horrible heart-rending scream. It was as if Buster had been shot with a harpoon. Engleburt shouted, "What's wrong?" And Buster roared, "Engleburt, my little feathery friend, save me from this Giant One! She's going to smoosh me!"

Engleburt didn't realize at first what was going on. It was dark. He looked around terrified, trying to see where the Giant One was. He certainly didn't want Buster to be smooshed. But he couldn't find any Giant One. He could still hear them singing—but way off to the northwest.

And then it dawned on him. Buster was having a bad dream.

"Wake up, wake up, Buster!"

But how can a penguin—so small, so weak, compared to a great blue whale—hope to wake up the huge behemoth?

Then—even as Buster kept crying and moaning and screaming in the middle of his awful nightmare—Engleburt had a great idea. He took a big breath, hoping his friend Buster wouldn't suddenly roll over and smoosh the life out of him, and he dove down under Buster to where his great fins met his gigantic side, just below his massive head. Penguins are very good underwater swimmers—as swift as any fish, and as agile in the water as an eagle is in the air.

Just as Buster began to roll and roar again Engleburt began tickling his whale-friend under his right fin. Engleburt hung on to Buster for dear life—as the whale rolled and cried and breached the water, sailing tremendously through the air and crashing back into the sea with a fabulous crack like the explosion of a big cannon.

Through all this the brave Engleburt hung on, and dug his beak into the soft flesh under Buster's fin.

Now whales are mammals. They don't have scales. They have warm blood. They should be ticklish, thought Engleburt.

He kept tickling Buster but he felt his own strength start to go. He knew that if Buster plunged into the deep and sounded—that is, headed for the bottom of the sea—he was lost, he could not hold on any longer, maybe he would drown.

But just as he was thinking these terrible thoughts, Buster started rolling with laughter, and all of his many tons of blubber started shaking like a great dish of jello.

"Ho, ho, ha, ha, hee, hee, ha, ha!!!" laughed Buster. Then fully awake he cried out, "Stop tickling me, you crazy penguin! Stop, stop!!"

But Engleburt dug his beak even deeper and wiggled his head furiously from side to side. He wanted to make absolutely sure that Buster was awake.

"Ha, ha, ha, ha!!! Stop or I'll pee!"

Then suddenly Engleburt felt a firehose-powerful jet of warm liquid. "Uh-oh," he said, "this whale has peed on me! I don't want anymore of that!"

So Engleburt let go. Buster calmed down. And then, songs of the Giant Ones or not, they both fell into the deepest, sweetest sleep imaginable.

# Meeting the Giant Ones

 THE NEXT morning the sea was very calm. It was a hot day. Overhead a few white seagulls circled lazily in the still air. Engleburt and Buster had forgotten about their bad dreams and about what they imagined they heard and saw the night before.
But then they heard the song again!

We are the Giant Ones
The Giant Ones, the Giant Ones!
We are the Giant Ones
We're so tall
You can never tell
Where we begin or end!
BEEEEEEP!!!

And this time there could be no mistake. They saw the Giant Ones stomping through the water as if the Atlantic Ocean was just a wading pool. Each step a Giant One took splashed water hundreds of feet into the air. And soon Engleburt and Buster were struggling against the great waves thrown up by the Giant Ones' frolicking.

These Giant Ones were big women dressed in sort of cave-people's style clothes. They wore gigantic furs—maybe sewn together from the skins of thousands of seals. They were so tall their heads disappeared into the sky. And the ocean was so deep that their feet disappeared into the water. All that Engleburt and Buster could see was from the Giant Ones' knees to their shoulders. That's why their song made so much sense: "You can never tell where we begin or end!"

"Wow," muttered Buster.

"Yeah, wow," repeated Engleburt.

The Giant Ones—six of them—were getting closer and closer. But these big women didn't seem to notice the blue whale or the little penguin at all. Even though Buster was a member of the species thought to be the biggest ever to exist on earth, it was clear he was just like a little toy fish next to these great huge Giant Ones.

Engleburt said, "How about you stay real still, pretend you're a rock or something, and when they get close I'll jump up on one of them and try to climb to the top?"

"You're crazy," Buster said. "I think you should take a big breath and I'll sound to the deepest water I can get to and then we'll swim out of here at full speed."

"Nonsense," answered Engleburt. "Why do you think these big people are bad? I want to meet them! Besides, if I fall, they are so tall that during the time it takes me to fall down, you can position yourself right under me."

"Come on," said Buster angrily. "If you fall from the top of one of those girls, you'll be traveling at such a speed you'll go right through me. Let's get out of here."

Then the bird and the whale got into a terrible argument. They shouted at each other. Buster splashed his flukes in the water. Engleburt screeched at the top of his lungs. They made such a commotion that one of the Giant Ones noticed something going on in the water beneath her knees.

She said, "HEY, MARTHA! LOOK DOWN THERE! DO YOU SEE WHAT I SEE?"

Whenever a Giant One talked, even quietly, it made a big roar that you could hear for miles.

"LOOKS LIKE MY LOST BATH TOY," said Martha peering down at Buster. She didn't see Engleburt at all.

At that, Martha's friend Virginia bent over and scooped Buster up in her right hand palm.

The last words that Engleburt heard Buster say as he was whisked up on that Giant's hand ascending like a swift super elevator were: "Uh-oh, we've been spotted!"

"I guess so," Engleburt said meekly.

Engleburt began swimming in circles near Martha's legs. He kept butting his head into her, nibbling at her calves with his beak, trying to get her attention. But he was so small that even with all his strength Martha didn't notice. Meanwhile, high in the sky Buster got a good look at Martha's face.

It was a kind face, a gentle face, a sweet face, the kind of face you hardly ever see on earth but hope you will meet. And here it was, high in the sky.

Buster felt safe. But he also knew that he had to get back in the water. It isn't possible for a whale to be out of water very long. His skin dries up and he overheats and he dies. But Martha seemed to understand this, because she said to Virginia, "HEY, THIS IS NO TOY! THIS CREATURE IS ALIVE! IT'S A REAL LIVING ITSY-BITSY WHALE!" And she immediately stooped down and put Buster back in the ocean.

She put Buster back with exceeding care. Slowly she lowered her hand and let the water flood into her palm and then she opened her fingers and with her thumb gave Buster the slightest nudge urging him to swim away.

Engleburt saw his chance at that moment. He was dying for some great adventure. And as Buster swam out Engleburt swam in. When they passed each other, Engleburt said, "My turn to take a look up there." Engleburt was a bird but he couldn't fly—this would be his first chance to get a bird's-eye view of things.

Buster was no longer afraid for his friend. So he just swam off a few hundred yards to the side and lolled in the warm South Atlantic waters.

Engleburt hung on to Martha's little finger for dear life. He felt like he was crunched in a washing machine. He was inside her fist. She didn't know he was there. But she felt something in her hand—something feathery and tiny. She brought her hand to her right eye. Engleburt looked into that huge blue shiny orb. And Martha peered down into her hand, squinting in the bright tropical sun. She focussed hard and finally made out the details of this tiny tiny animal she was carrying.

"WOULD YOU BELIEVE!" she laughed, "A PENGUIN!!"

"A PENGUIN!" Virginia echoed unbelievingly. "HOW COULD THAT BE? THIS IS NOT THE ANTARCTIC OCEAN OR THE GALAPAGOS ISLANDS OR THE COAST OF AFRICA!"—all places where penguins live—"SO WHAT'S HE DOING HERE?"

"I swam here with my friend Buster the whale," Engleburt shouted in his loudest squeak.

"SO THAT WAS YOUR 'BATH TOY' " Martha said to Virginia.

# Talking to the Giant Ones

 BURSTING with excitement, Engleburt asked Virginia, "How many of you are there? Where do you live? What are your names? How tall are you? How did you get to be so big? Do you have a mother? How does your kind of species of animal multiply?" And those were only a few of the questions crowding forward in Engleburt's brain like a big swarm of bees trying to get out of their hive.

"Hold on, my little orange-toed bird," Virginia said in her quietest, most soothing voice. "We can only answer one question at a time."

"Ok," replied Engleburt. "Tell me what you can."

Martha began.

"We are called 'The Giant Ones' and we live in the Atlantic Ocean right off the coast of eastern Brazil—a few hundred miles off the city of Recife, just south of the equator. There are twelve of us."

"Where are the others? Are you sisters?" Somehow Engleburt knew there were no male Giant Ones. "Can I meet all of you?"

"Our sisters are far away fishing. They use big palm trees as fishing brooms. They sweep the ocean and catch the fish in the palm fronds. I don't think you can meet them now."

"Can we go with you?"

"No. We Giant Ones never let any other kinds of creatures accompany us on our mysterious journies."

"Mysterious journies? What do you mean?" Engleburt asked full of curiosity.

"We keep the clouds moving, we make sure the ocean stays in its basins, we watch out for mistakes in the weather," Virginia said. "Once we lived on land in a continent called Atlantis. But long ago that continent sank into the sea. As it sank so slowly we got bigger and bigger step by step. And so now we still walk on our familiar Atlantis streets—but those streets are hundreds of feet below us on the ocean floor."

"Wow," whispered Engleburt.

"And we don't multiply—we stay as we are. We live forever. And as for our mothers we have never had even a single one."

Engleburt could hardly believe his ears. It was all so different than the way he thought things were. He even started to feel a little afraid again. But Martha and Virginia were so gentle, even as they were so gigantic. Soon Engleburt's fears faded.

Then he said: "My friend Buster and I are headed for the Bahamas where he is meeting a lot of whales for a conference. I am looking for a warm tropical island to live on. Can you recommend any?"

"Four hundred miles east of here is St. Paul Rock."

"St. Paul Rock? No, I don't want a rock. I want an island full of palm trees and birds of paradise and purple sunsets. So thanks anyway but I'll keep looking."

Then there was a pause in the conversation.

Overhead the sun was hot.

Engleburt looked down from Martha's shoulder where he was standing. The descent was so steep he got dizzy just looking. And on the shiny ocean surface he could barely make out a tiny gray smudge. He knew it was Buster. And he was homesick for his friend and for the gentle rocking of the sea.

"Please put me down now," he said.

And the next thing he knew he was flapping wings flying down while still being carried in Martha's great hand and before he knew it he was in the ocean next to Buster.

When Engleburt turned his eyes up the Giant Ones were already moving away through the warm sea. They had started singing again, and Buster and Engleburt could hear their great booming chorus:

> We are the Giant Ones
> The Giant Ones, the Giant Ones. . . .

Neither Buster nor Engleburt nor the Giant Ones themselves knew what was soon to befall those huge gentle Atlantan women. For not too many days after leaving Engleburt the greatest wind imaginable tore at those twelve Giant Women pulling them to pieces but not killing them. Instead they were transformed into millions and millions and millions of krill—a kind of small shrimp swimming through the seas nourishing birds and fish alike. And even today sometimes in a great school of krill, if you listen very carefully, you might hear this song:

> We were the Giant Ones
> The Giant Ones, the Giant Ones
> We were the Giant Ones
> But now we're so small
> You can never tell
> If we exist or not!
> BLEEEEEEP!!

# Old Elmer Tortoise of St. Paul Rock

CURIOSITY got the better of Engleburt. He thought that maybe Martha the Giant One knew what she was talking about.

"Let's check out St. Paul Rock," Engleburt said. "It might be the island I'm looking for."

Actually Engleburt was a little tired of traveling. He had never been at sea this long before. He was starting to miss his old penguin friends. He loved Buster, of course, and he enjoyed all the things that had happened to them, but he needed to settle down. He needed to have some firm ground to put his orange feet on. He wanted to build a nest—and that was not possible on the slippery skin of a great sea mammal. Especially a mammal that dove under water every once in a while.

"Maybe St. Paul Rock isn't so rocky after all," Engleburt hoped. "There may be a few palm trees there, don't you think? And anyway, penguins like rocks—our nests are built out of rocks."

Buster didn't answer. He just kept swimming.

"Do you know why?" Engleburt asked.

"Why what?" answered Buster, who wasn't really listening to the conversation of his friend.

The big whale was just enjoying the warm water sloshing

against his very sensitive skin. Whales are huge, but their skin is as sensitive as a little baby's cheek.

"Why we penguins don't use twigs and leaves to build our nests."

"That's cinchy," Buster answered. "Do you think just because I'm big I'm stupid?"

"Well, no," Engleburt said. "But tell me the answer, if you think you're so smart."

Buster waved his giant flukes.

"Do you know the answer yourself?" he asked Engleburt.

"Of course I do. I'm a penguin. I've seen the penguins in my colony build plenty of nests. When I'm ready to mate I'll build a nest."

"Ok, you know the answer and I know the answer. So let's drop the subject," said Buster, a little irritated.

"No," said Engleburt. "I bet you don't know the answer?"

"How much you wanna bet?" Buster shot back.

"A big, fat oyster."

"You're on," said the whale.

"So?" asked Engleburt again.

By this time they were getting close to St. Paul Rock. It was a single blue black slab of rock slanting up from the flat surface of the sea. It looked very uninviting.

"There it is!" shouted Engleburt.

"Yep, that's old St. Paul Rock all right," replied Buster.

They turned straight for the Rock and Buster increased his speed.

As they swam along Engleburt piped up, "So why do we penguins build our nests from rocks?"

"Because you crazy birds love hard cold stones!" Buster answered.

"Ehhhhhhh!" buzzed Engleburt. "The whale's wrong. A big fat oyster goes to Engleburt the penguin." He flapped his wings as he shouted: "The answer is, there's nothing else in Antarctica to build nests from."

"Aw, I don't care about a silly oyster," Buster burst out.

By this time they were at St. Paul Rock. And indeed it was just a bare rock. Not a tree, not a bush, not a twig. And it was very hot there on the equator.

They were just about to swim away when a voice from St. Paul Rock stopped them.

"Hello there, friends."

Engleburt squinted into the reflection of the sun sparkling off the wet Rock. On its very edge sat a big tortoise. Not a sea turtle, mind you, but a tortoise.

"Come over here," said the tortoise. "My name's Elmer, and I'm older than both of you combined and squared," he declared. "Oh, yes, and I rarely see anyone at all. But I am very talkative."

"I can see that," Buster said.

"We don't have much time," Engleburt added.

"I remember when I used to live on the other side of the great South American continent," Elmer orated.

"Really?" said Engleburt.

"Oh, yes, my feathered friend. I used to live on the Galápagos Islands. And I know exactly who you are. You are an Adélie Penguin, of the phylum verterbrata, class aves, order sphenisciformes, family spheniscidae, genus and species pygoscelis adeliae. There are many other genus and species of penguins, seventeen to be exact. I have not met them all, but I know who you are. Oh, yes."

Buster and Engleburt were very impressed by the tortoise's wisdom and learning.

And once Elmer began lecturing he was very hard to stop.

"Oh, yes," he said, "I know all about the species and subspecies, the flora and fauna. In fact," Elmer said proudly, "I taught everything I know to an extraordinary young man who spent many hours with me when I used to live on the Galápagos Islands."

"Really?" Engleburt said, with a touch of disbelief in his voice.

"Oh, yes," Elmer replied slowly. "That boy came sailing in on the great ship Beagle. Let's see—it must have been more than

150 years ago now—when I was a young tortoise, barely more than 75 years old, just out of my teens. Well, that young Charlie was so curious. He wanted to know this and that and that and this. Oh, yes, I told him everything I knew, and everything I'd ever heard about from all the animals I'd talked to. I told that Charlie which animal came from where and what species followed what. We got to be such good friends. I was sad when young Charlie left the Galápagos.''

Buster and Engleburt could understand that.

Engleburt felt sorry for this tortoise whose shell was hard but whose heart was soft.

Obviously Elmer was lonely out here on desolate St. Paul Rock.

Buster signaled to Engleburt that they had to be on their way. But Engleburt wanted to keep Elmer company.

''How did you get from the Galápagos Islands to this place?'' Engleburt asked.

''Oh, yes,'' Elmer sighed. ''I was picked up from the Galápagos about 90 years ago. A whaling ship came by needing food. They used to pack in hundreds of tortoises just like me. We didn't need to be kept on ice. They would slaughter us for meat, one by one. Once aboard their whaler they put me in a terribly small compartment, a plain wood box. There were four other tortoises in there with me. Our quarters were indescribably crowded, unpleasant, and cruel. It was dark, damp, dirty—no place for a highly educated vertabrata reptilia chelonia testudinidae geochelone elephantopus like me.''

Elmer stopped his woeful tale and slowly blinked his enormous left eye.

''That's giant Galápagos tortoise to you.''

He paused. Buster was now interested in the tortoise's story. Buster knew about whalers.

''I couldn't see a thing,'' Elmer continued, ''but I knew we were heading into rough seas by the way my box rocked back and forth and up and down. I was full of dread. When would my time come? Even if by some miracle I escaped becoming a whaler's supper, I would spend the rest of my days—and I had many days left—in a zoo.''

Were those tears filling the great tortoise's eyes?

''Oh, yes, I was just remembering my many friends who were with me on that fatal last trip.''

Elmer turned his head from Engleburt and withdrew a little distance into his shell.

''Please pardon me.''

Yes, a big crystal clear tear formed in the corner of each of Elmer's eyes.

Engleburt didn't know what to say. He tentatively raised one of his wings in a gesture of reassurance. Elmer was so much older, so much wiser, than he. And yet Engleburt felt like a parent to this big, highly educated tortoise. He wanted to protect Elmer, to make some of his pain go away.

''It is a terrible thing to remember all those days of cruelty,'' Elmer said. ''How little water there was and less food. How the whalers had no regard for our lives at all.''

''Not to mention the lives of whales!'' roared Buster, unable at last to hold his anger in another second.

''I hate, hate, hate, hate whalers!'' the gentle blue whale yelled.

The whole equatorial sea shook with Buster's rage.

He beat the surface of the ocean with his flukes until the waters were all foam. Slowly Buster calmed down, his indignation spent.

''If I weren't a peace-loving mammal I'd hunt the hunters and sink every last one of their ships.''

But Buster knew whaling ships these days are made of steel, armed with harpoon guns capable of destroying with one blast even such a magnificent animal as he.

Then the three of them fell silent.

They considered the fate of the animals.

Not only tortoises and whales, but other species too. Birds and gorillas, tiny fish and even insects.

They listened to the silence of the sea as the sun beat down on them.

Then Elmer went on.

"Oh, yes, I was lucky," he said. "The rocking I felt was preface to a storm—not just an ordinary blow but a hurricane. The whaling ship lost sails and masts. Finally she lost her rudder and was pushed rudely toward this rock. She was bashed to splinters. All aboard her drowned, except for me and four whalers."

"What did you do?" Engleburt asked.

"I saved myself."

"And the other tortoises?"

"By the time of the hurricane only a few of us were left. I assume the others were swept overboard and lost. We're not sea turtles, you know. I was lucky. As soon as my box broke open I felt this very rock beneath my feet. I crawled ashore. When the storm ended I slipped into the shallow waters and waited."

"Waited?" Engleburt asked.

"Oh, yes. I waited them out, those few surviving sailors. It didn't take too long—less than a month. They had no water. They all died. It was gruesome. Long ago I pushed their bones into the sea. Many years ago."

Again Elmer paused.

"I never saw another of my kind, not then, not now."

"So you've lived all alone here?" Engleburt asked.

"All alone."

This time Buster broke the silence.

"I don't feel sorry for the whaling men. I don't feel sorry for them at all."

Elmer turned his wise head to Buster. He extended his neck a far distance outside his shell. He opened his mouth as if to speak, but no words came out.

It was a strange sight on St. Paul Rock. An old tortoise on the flat ledge of stone. A giant blue whale snug up close to shore. An Adélie penguin sitting on the edge of the rock. All of them intent on their silence.

Engleburt felt it was better not to talk at this moment. He wanted to let Buster's feelings take their own course. Engleburt knew the time would come when things would feel normal again.

After a few minutes, Elmer spoke up.

"And here I am still. Barely eking out an existence eating mussels and crabs. And thinking about my old—"

"Speaking of molluscs," Engleburt interrupted, "you owe me a fat oyster, Buster."

Elmer didn't even stop when Engleburt began.

"—friend young Charlie. I know you have to be on your way. I'd come along with you, but after so many years I'm used to my hermit's life here on this rock. And I swore a solemn oath to myself never to set foot on the sea again after that awful experience on the whaling ship. So here I will stay until I live out my full 400 years."

Elmer stood up as high as he could on his four stubby feet. He surveyed his kingdom.

"If you ever come this way again, I would be most happy to entertain you, oh yes. And to tell you many things you might not otherwise know."

But in his heart Elmer knew these travelers would not return.

"Come on," Buster whispered to Engleburt, "let's make waves."

Engleburt cast an eye back on Elmer.

He felt a deep warmth for the old Galápagos tortoise. Maybe he even felt sorry for him.

But Elmer didn't feel sorry for himself.

He kept on talking.

"Oh, yes, those were the days . . ."

Soon Elmer's voice trailed off blending in with the rush of the sea as penguin and whale moved steadily northward. It was not long before St. Paul Rock sunk over the horizon.

Suddenly, issuing as great a shriek as Engleburt had ever in his whole life heard, Buster sounded.

Engleburt felt a surge of terror as his big friend vanished into the deep.

But after 30 seconds the big blue whale reappeared. In his baleen he displayed dozens of fat delicious oysters.

"When this whale loses a bet," Buster proudly declaimed, "this whale pays off."

# Buster Leaves

ENGLEBURT and Buster swam north, away from the old tortoise and St. Paul Rock. They swam for two days. Soon enough they reached an area just off the coast of Venezuela.

While swimming they usually talked and talked.

They would talk about the fish they saw. Or about the weather. Or about their experiences with each other.

But during these two days they were very quiet.

There was a reason.

Buster knew that soon he would have to leave his friend Engleburt and go on alone to the Bahamas. And Engleburt knew the same thing.

It made them both very very sad.

"But what can I do?" Buster burst out suddenly. "I have to go and meet all the other blue whales! We meet like this only once every five years—and every living blue whale in the whole wide world swims to our secret meeting place—an underwater cave in the Bahamas."

"I know, I know," said Engleburt. "But still it makes me sad."

They swam on the rest of the day without talking to each other again.

Sometimes when friends are very close to each other, they don't have to say much to communicate. They communicate just by being together. Engleburt knew that Buster would have to go to the big whale convention in the Bahamas. There was nothing he could do to stop it. And Buster knew that also. Anyway, Buster was looking forward to seeing all his whale friends and relations. He would see his mother and father again, and his brothers and sisters, and cousins, and aunts and uncles, and second cousins, and grandmothers and grandfathers. Not to mention all the other friends and relations not listed. He hoped that everyone he loved would be all right. Sometimes terrible things happen—especially to whales.

All of these thoughts were going through Buster's mind.

Suddenly, Engleburt broke the silence.

"Hey," he said, "why not take me with you? I'd love to meet your family and friends."

Buster thought it over a long slow minute before he answered. He didn't want to hurt his penguin friend's feelings. But he knew Engleburt would be really out of place among all those huge blue whales. And he knew that the whales would be socializing with each other in ways that only whales know how to do.

"I'd love to take you with me, but not this time."

"Oh, please," Engleburt pleaded, a tear running down his feathery cheek.

Then Buster took his left flipper and picked little Engleburt up, and held him right next to his big gray eye.

"I just can't. I just can't."

It was very sad.

The two friends from different species loved each other more than words can tell.

They each wondered if they would ever see each other again.

And they knew they had to go their different ways.

"I'll tell you what," said Buster. "After the convention, I'll come to your island and spend a few days with you."

"Terrific," said Engleburt happily. "But I don't know which island I'm going to. How will you find me?"

"I'll search all the islands of the Caribbean Sea. You make a big white flag with an orange circle in the middle—and fly that flag from the highest point on your island's western beach—that's the side of the island where the sun sets into the sea."

"Ok, I will," said Engleburt. "And you promise you'll come?"

"Promise," replied Buster.

They swam on a little bit longer. They swam slowly, and they bounced into each other playfully. Engleburt dived down underneath Buster and made spirals around the vast girth of his giant friend. Buster, for his part, sang high-pitched whale songs—songs of admiration and love for his small friend.

They were very happy together.

But their happiness was coming to a close—soon they would have to part. Engleburt wondered whether he would ever see Buster again. He knew that friends always promise to see each other even when they move to a new neighborhood, city, or country. But he also knew those promises were mostly broken. Like so many before him, Engleburt thought, in my case it will be different. I will see my friend again, I think.

Buster was thinking the same thoughts, making the same promises to himself.

Then, after a long period of silence, Buster said aloud, "Here we are at Barbados. I have to go northwest now at full speed."

"I understand," said Engleburt.

The penguin couldn't say anymore. His throat was all stopped up.

"I know how you feel," said Buster. "I feel the same way."

"It's ok," Engleburt said. "I'll stay in this vicinity and look for my island around here."

"I bet you'll find the perfect island, and all your dreams will come true."

Buster sounded cheerier than he really was.

"I hope so," piped Engleburt in a small voice tinged with tears.

Both of them were trying to hide their feelings of sadness. But the strategy didn't work. Strong feelings always have their ways of getting out. Engleburt wanted to cry but couldn't because he was a bird and birds can't shed tears, but Buster as a mammal had no such limitation.

Soon Buster's tears were visible as great rivers of salty liquid poured from his large eyes as big as a computer's screen. These tears mingled with the warm saltiness of the Caribbean Sea. Then Buster gave out one gigantic tearful sigh. Engleburt was right underneath Buster's left eye—and the blue whale's torrent of tears fell on the penguin like a warm salty shower. If they weren't both so sad they would've laughed at the scene.

Finally, Engleburt said, "But what are we crying about? After all, think how lucky we are to have each other as friends. And think what a great trip we've had together. And think how soon it will be when we shall see each other again."

He was really trying very hard to cheer himself up.

Deep in his heart he was plenty scared that he'd never see his whale friend again. And he was frightened of being on his own. Down in Antarctica he made a big thing of being independent, even fearless. He always bragged how he could get along all by himself. But now, about to be really alone, he knew he needed friends. And he knew he was about to be separated from the second best friend he'd ever had. The best was Andy, his penguin buddy still in Antarctica.

Buster waved once with his left flipper, and then he rolled over and waved once with his right flipper, and then with a giant crash of his flukes he roared off to the northwest, leaving a trail of salty tears behind him.

Engleburt watched him go.

Once, when Buster was about a mile away, he stopped, dove deep down so that he could gain momentum on his upward acceleration and then at last the blue whale breached the sea's surface with tremendous speed, and launching himself high into the air screamed "Engleburrrrt!!!!" with all his mighty might as he came crashing back down to the water. Engleburt heard this sad farewell and saw the foamy impact of Buster's immense bulk as it splashed into the water. Engleburt paid attention with his whole heart as the sound and sight of his good friend faded away.

Engleburt saw some seagulls circling in the blue warm Caribbean sky above where he thought Buster might be. But then, too soon, the gulls too vanished.

Engleburt felt how warm the water was around him.

He tried to concentrate his mind on what he had accomplished, not on Buster's departure.

He swam on quietly.

He felt the support of the bouyant ocean all around him.

He felt good about himself.

He really had done it!

He had made his way from Antarctica across the Equator to the warm northern tropics.

He was sad, but he was also happy.

Now what he had to do was to find his very own island.

# Searching for Real Estate

ENGLEBURT swam for a few days looking at various islands. Some were too big, some were too small, some didn't have enough vegetation, some were too windy, and some had wild animals on them who looked like they would love to eat a penguin.

There was one island Engleburt thought would be perfect. It had a nice little bay of shallow warm water full of delicious fish and juicy shrimps.

Engleburt just loved shrimps.

There were palm trees growing right down to the water. The sand was clean. And there were many caves along a rocky stretch of beach. These caves were important because if Engleburt brought other penguins up from Antarctica they would want places to build their nests and raise their young.

In Antarctica they use small rocks and pebbles to build their nests—because only rocks are handy in that dark, cold place where trees and shrubbery just can't grow. So Engleburt was glad to find a rocky place on the island that would duplicate some of the conditions of Antarctica, but still be very warm and comfortable.

Engleburt was so happy he just lay down on the beach of this perfect island, closed his eyes, and fell into a deep but nicely dreamy sleep.

The next thing he knew, ten brown chattering monkeys were tugging at him, plucking off his feathers, trying to take him away God knows where.

"Hey," Engleburt shouted full of surprise. "Quit that! I'm not supper!"

But the monkeys didn't understand a word he squeaked. They didn't speak Engleburt's language. Unlike Buster, these monkeys had never visited the south pole. All they saw in Engleburt was bird meat.

Luckily Engleburt was able to pull himself free. As soon as he did so he ran straight for the ocean.

Monkeys don't like to swim. And penguins swim like the wind.

So Engleburt got away.

But he knew that this "perfect island" was not for him or his kind.

For two days he kept searching the Caribbean. If it weren't so warm and sunny he might have gotten discouraged.

He tried many islands cautiously—he didn't want to meet any more hungry monkeys or whatever other animals might be residing there with a big appetite for bird meat.

Finally he found the right island.

It was not too big, it was not too small. And it had the perfect name, Martinique.

Martinique was a lively place.

There were humans there.

Engleburt remembered how nice humans were to him when he fell in the ice pit on Antarctica.

And, believe it or not, as Engleburt swam up and down the beachline, he saw John and Veeny—the very people who rescued him from the ice pit. He swam right up to them and jumped into Veeny's arms.

She was so surprised, she let out a great big scream. "Yiiikes!!!" And she fell backwards into the water making a big splash.

John laughed and laughed.

"Don't you recognize him?" he scolded Veeny as he helped her to her feet. "That's our very own penguin from Antarctica."

"You mean—?"

"Yes, the one we pulled out of the crevasse."

"How can you be sure," Veeny asked suspiciously. She didn't like getting her hair wet.

"Well, what other penguin would be swimming offshore Club Med in Martinique and jump right up into your arms? I might add, that's exactly the same jump he made down in Antarctica."

Veeny wasn't convinced.

But Engleburt began making such enthusiastic squeaks that she began to feel that maybe John was right.

"Hello," she said. "Are you my penguin from the south pole?"

Engleburt squeaked as loud as his avian lungs let him.

"I guess you're right, John," said Veeny. "The penguin squeaks a convincing story."

The two humans looked at each other with a wonderfully pleased expression in their eyes. Then their pleasure mixed in with a questioning look.

"But what's he doing here?"

"And how did he get here?"

Engleburt was only too ready to supply the answer.

He squeaked.

"I swam. I was helped by Buster my blue whale friend. I always wanted to live in the tropics. I hate cold weather. I hate Antarctica. I mean the place, not my good old aunt."

Then Engleburt told them the whole story. He left out no detail, including the Giant Ones and Gertrude and Angelina, the mommy and baby sharks, and Old Elmer Tortoise of St. Paul Rock.

Little did Engleburt know as he squeaked and flapped his wings, and ran up and down the beach demonstrating this and that incident from his great adventures that neither John nor Veeny could understand a word of Penguin.

All they knew was that their old friend from the south pole was very excited and having lots of fun.

# Settling in on Martinique

MARTINIQUE was perfect—but it had its problems too. Mainly that people lived there—many many people. Local people and tourists.

And there was a big volcano, Mt. Pelée.

Mt. Pelée was asleep when Engleburt arrived. But 86 years earlier it had erupted with great and awesome force, killing many people and burning many villages.

Engleburt didn't know any of this history. He just looked up at the northern end of the island in the middle of the tropics and saw, high on its slopes, snow—and he thought, ''Well, if I ever get homesick, I can climb that big mountain and frolic in the snow.''

Engleburt was thinking these thoughts while he lay in a human bed in John and Veeny's hotel room at Club Med on Martinique.

You see, the two scientists on vacation decided to take Engleburt with them. And Engleburt was more than willing. He trusted them, he was tired from all his travels, he could use a few days rest and recreation.

They fed Engleburt fresh flounder and pompano. Engleburt entertained all of the Club Med guests by doing swimming tricks in the pool.

Many of the guests had seen trained seals and dolphins and

even killer whales. But no one had ever seen an untrained, totally wild penguin so willing to show off his amazing swimming skills.

Engleburt swam at incredible speeds underwater, flipped over backwards from the high diving board, performing somersaults in the air. He leaped out of the pool and dove through hoops made from automobile inner tubes.

He was a big hit.

And he enjoyed every minute of it.

Veeny decided to experiment. She ordered two shrimp cocktails from the Club Med restaurant. Then she set one cocktail on a tray next to the pool. She took the other one on her lap and began to eat it very daintily. She gestured to Engleburt showing him how to eat the shrimp properly.

Engleburt watched intently as Veeny dipped the fat end of the shrimp into the red cocktail sauce. Then she daintily put the shrimp into her mouth, careful not to eat the tail which was still in its hard shell.

This was not the way Engleburt liked to eat shrimp. He gobbled down twenty at a time, shells and all. He liked to crunch them in his mouth and take in big gulps of salt water from the ocean too.

But he understood what Veeny wanted him to do. And he wanted to please his human friend.

So Engleburt deftly flipped the shrimp in the air with the tip of his beak and he caught it fat side up, nibbled off the unshelled portion and as daintily as a princess he deposited the tail with the shell on the ledge by the side of the pool.

The vacationers lounging there were amazed.

They laughed.

They applauded.

And so in this entertaining way Engleburt spent five glorious days with John and Veeny.

But then he had to get down to work.

He looked around and saw a group of pigeons eating left-over food scraps around the outdoor pool. Engleburt approached the pigeons hoping they would understand Penguin.

He began to squeak to them, and sure enough, one old gray pigeon came over and said, "What do you want?"

Engleburt answered, "Are any of you carrier pigeons—or do you know where I can find a carrier pigeon?"

The old gray pigeon said, "Why do you want to know?"

Engleburt summarized his whole life's story.

"I want to live in the tropics, but I don't want to live alone."

"So you want a pigeon to fly to Antarctica and see if any other penguins want to come up here to live with you?"

"You got it," Engleburt said.

"I'm a carrier pigeon—and the best of them all," the old gray pigeon said. "My name's Max."

"Glad to meet you." Engleburt held out his right wing and Max pecked gently at it. So they exchanged greetings.

"The best of them all, yes sir, but I'll never fly long distance again."

"Why not?"

"I'm glad you asked. I'll tell you my story."

# Max's Story

"WHEN I WAS a young bird, I liked far-away places. That's why I decided to be a carrier pigeon and go to carrier pigeon training school. I got my direction diploma when I was two years old.

"The first place I went was from Martinique to where I was born across the water in Mexico and then on to Hawaii. I had to go to Hawaii direct, of course it's all open water—but I was a terrifically strong bird. From Hawaii I flew to Washington Island—a very small place. On Washington Island I met a beautiful pigeon, we fell in love, and had three chicks together.

"She raised two of the brood herself, but one came with me back here."

"That's me," shouted a white pigeon pecking at a piece of pie crust poolside.

"On Washington Island I met a scientist, name of Dr. Perkins, who wanted to send me on a long mission to a friend of his in Windham, Australia. Dr. Perkins wanted me to carry a very small but crucially important fossil that he just wouldn't trust to any human method of transport—like airmail or Federal Express.

"On the way to Australia I stopped for rest at Rotuma Island—that's in the middle of the Pacific near New Caledonia, do you know the place?''

Engleburt shook his head no. The Pacific Ocean itself was unknown to him.

''Well, guess what happened. While I was resting at Rotuma, a crazy drunk hunter, after parrots, shot into the tree I was in and broke a branch above me. The branch crashed down onto my head and knocked me unconscious. I fell through the branches of the tree—and I would've been killed if a little twig hadn't caught hold of the tiny pouch carrying Dr. Perkins's fossil.''

''How do you know all this happened to you the way you're telling it to me if you were unconscious?'' Engleburt asked. Engleburt had learned to be very skeptical of tall stories.

''My daughter Riley''—(''That's me you see'' piped up the pie crust eating pigeon)—''saw the whole thing—she was sitting in an adjoining tree.''

Engleburt didn't know what to say.

''Anyway the most terrible thing to ever happen to a carrier pigeon happened to me on that day.''

''What was that?'' asked Engleburt.

''When the branch hit my head it knocked right out of my system every last thing I learned at carrier school. I couldn't find my way back to Washington Island—no less go on to Australia or get back to Martinique.''

''Pop's lucky I'm so plucky,'' said Riley.

''Sure am,'' smiled the old gray ex-carrier pigeon. ''From that day on, I've been following my daughter. I followed her all the way to Australia and all the way back home here.''

Engleburt was very glad to meet such a brave and kind and loving family. Although he was sad that Max couldn't go on distant missions alone anymore.

Engleburt said to Max, ''Do you think Riley would fly to Antarctica and tell my friends to come on up here to live?''

''Oh, no,'' Max said, ''I need Riley right here next to me. I'm getting old now and I want to rest where it's warm.''

''Oh, please, Dad, I'd be so glad!'' Riley sang. She was very enthusiastic about the prospect of a big flight south. But her father was adamant. He just wouldn't let her go.

# Hunting for Pigeons in a Friendly Way

SOON ENOUGH Max, exhausted from telling his story, and old as he was, sank down very low and closed his eyes.

"Pop's asleep, don't make a peep."

Riley forgot that Engleburt—bird though he was— could not fly. For as soon as she began talking she took off. But when she looked back all she saw was Engleburt running and wildly flapping his wings gesturing for her to slow down.

"Ooops, poops" Riley said apologetically swooping back to where Engleburt was.

Riley started out again, this time combining little short bursts of flight with backward glances to make sure Engleburt was following.

After fifteen minutes of this stop-and-go journey the penguin and the pigeon were deep into the rain forest of Martinique—a green jungle world full of parrot cries, giant ferns, towering palm trees, junipers, and live oaks. Engleburt had never seen such a world.

He was more than a little frightened.

Since he couldn't fly, Engleburt had to step across the mossy, soft, spongy rain forest floor. He saw—or thought he saw—giant insects, bees as big as sparrows, and long slithering snakes (all of which turned out to be creepy thick brown-barked vines). Still, Engleburt was sure that there were snakes there, he just knew there were.

Then suddenly he saw in front of him the two legs of a giant gorilla.

He stopped frozen in his tracks. He looked up, his penguin heart beating furiously.

Then, relief.

What he saw were two great trees meeting in the jungle canopy over his head. The ''gorilla legs'' were only the tree trunks.

But there were real monkeys.

Chattering little beasts, curious about the new visitor to their jungle, their brown shapes swinging through the jungle canopy with delight, they hung onto branches and vines—and they loved running up and down the big ''gorilla legs.''

On and on Riley led Engleburt deeper and deeper into the forest.

Soon Engleburt felt his legs turning to rubber. He just couldn't walk through this spongy-bottomed world another step. He was exhausted.

''Riley,'' he said wearily, ''I have to take a nap. I can't go on even two more steps.''

Riley answered, ''Don't despair, we're almost there! We must press on, and on and on—for if my father wakes and finds I'm gone, I'll wish I had been born a swan! Come on, come on, press on, press on!''

But Engleburt wasn't listening.

Engleburt was looking around fearful of footsteps he thought he heard behind him.

He stopped.

He peered around. And then he heard a great roar. He saw the two giant ''gorilla legs'' walking down the green pathway and smooshing down trees.

Engleburt shouted, ''Riley! Riley! I told you I saw a giant gorilla. He's here, he's going to smoosh me! Help, oh please,

Riley, help me! Riley! Riley! Riley!''

The sound of his own shout for help drifted off and Engleburt woke up.

It was a nightmare.

There was no giant gorilla, only the vast fans of huge ferns and the crying of a million exotic birds and insects.

But then he got really scared when he looked around and Riley was nowhere in sight.

Frantically Engleburt started running this way and that way looking for Riley.

He shouted her name for real—but the only answers he got were the laughing taunts of the little brown monkeys swinging in the branches far over his head.

Riley hadn't noticed that Engleburt fell asleep. She was already far ahead in a small clearing conferring with dozens of her pigeon friends. When she turned around to introduce a special pigeon named Bruce to Engleburt, Riley was shocked to discover that Engleburt had vanished.

Now it was Riley's turn to worry.

Had Engleburt been swallowed by a boa constrictor? Had he gotten his wings tangled in sticky vines? Could it possibly be that the rain forest was the home of a giant gorilla? Did one of the hairy spiders who live under rocks nip at Engleburt's toes injecting paralyzing poison into him? Or maybe, Riley thought, Engleburt simply fell asleep. She remembered how tired Engleburt said he was.

So she sang out to her friend, ''Bruce, hang loose, I gotta go back to chase the goose.''

Meanwhile Engleburt had ventured far from where he had fallen asleep—and he was totally lost. But he was not the kind of penguin to get depressed. He decided he would sing a song—and hoped that Riley, or some helpful animal or human, would hear him.

He remembered how he had fallen into the ice pit back in Antarctica; he remembered the time that Gertrude had charged at him and Buster with her rows and rows of sharp shiny white teeth.

As soon as Engleburt thought of Buster, he burst out crying.

The sound of Engleburt's sobbing caught Riley's attention. She was not far away, but the thickness of the rain forest had prevented her from seeing Engleburt. She soon located him. Carrier pigeons are extremely skilled at locations.

"Cheer up, my friend, your misery's at an end. Riley's here, have no fear."

"Oh, Riley!" shouted Engleburt. "I wasn't so afraid. I was thinking of an old friend I miss."

Riley carefully led Engleburt back to the conference of pigeons. There she introduced him to Bruce.

Engleburt explained his need.

Bruce agreed to make the trip to Antarctica.

# The Long Wait

EARLY THE next morning all the pigeons of the forest gathered around to watch Bruce set off on his long journey. None of them had ever flown so many miles. It was more than 7,000 miles one way. That makes it more than 14,000 miles round trip. It would take Bruce many weeks to cover that kind of distance.

And the journey was as dangerous as it was long.

Remember how much Gertrude and her sharp-toothed shark friends like fowl.

And the weather also can be foul.

But Bruce was not scared.

He looked forward to the adventure.

Engleburt had instructed him about who to look for when he arrived in the continent of endless ice. Engleburt was sure that some of his old penguin acquaintances would want to come north to the tropics after Bruce explained to them the advantages. And especially after Bruce told them how well Engleburt had made out in Martinique.

Engleburt knew that while Bruce was gone his work was cut out for him. He would ask Riley to help him find a proper spot to set up his penguin city, the tropical home of Antarctic penguins.

But Riley first had to make peace with Max, her father.

For Max woke up before Riley expected him to.

"Where's my daughter," he cried out with all his might.

But none of the other older pigeons knew.

Max wasn't worried so much as he was angry.

Riley had flown off before on her own.

And Max was the kind of daddy who kept a tight control on the whereabouts of his children—or at least of this one child on whom he relied.

But Max also knew it was useless looking for Riley.

She would come back when she would come back.

And having lost his own locating abilities he could not go off looking for her.

Max felt that Riley had gone into the jungle. He knew there were groups of young feral pigeons there. He had heard about their parties. Of how they flew around and around in tight circles just above the tree line. Of how they sang as they danced in the air. And of all the youthful, wild things they did.

So Max settled in for the night.

And sure enough, early the next morning—after Bruce had begun his fateful flight—Riley and Engleburt returned to Club Med and the company of Max.

Before her father could say a word, Riley began.

"Sorry, Dad, I know it's bad to leave you—that's sure to peeve you. But Engleburt, my friend, was at the end of his rope. Nope, I had no choice but to rejoice with the young pigeons of the jungle. We didn't bungle. Bruce is gone on his long flight. He will be flying day and night all the way south into the mouth of winter."

Engleburt interrupted.

"Bruce is bringing my message to my friends at home. He's telling them to come here to my new city, where all the penguins can live in warmth."

"Ok, ok," Max said both wearily and happily. "I'm just glad that Riley didn't desert her old dad."

"Oh, father, why do you bother to worry? Engleburt and I are in a hurry. This whole island we've got to span in order to fulfill Engleburt's plan."

Max smiled.

He was glad to see Riley so excited.

And he liked Engleburt.

"Go ahead, children," he said. "And I have a suggestion for you. I think on the northern end of the island, near the big mountain, you will find the right environment for your settlement."

"Why do you say that?" Engleburt asked.

"Because in the mountain there are caves, which I know penguins love, and on the mountain are rocks that will remind you of your home in Antarctica. The only difference is that on the mountain it can get very warm." Then, with a wise wink of his old pigeon eye, he added, "Sometimes too warm."

"It can never get too warm for me," replied Engleburt.

"We gotta go, don't be slow," Riley urged, tugging Engleburt's left wing.

So off they went to Mt. Pelée.

# The Great Volcano

THEY SAW the mountain from many miles away. Although it is only 4,429 feet high—which isn't so much compared to the Rocky Mountains or the Himalayas—Mt. Pelée was still the highest place on Martinique. Its great gray rocky surface dominated the whole northern end of the island. On its lower slopes was a dense tropical rain forest consisting of giant ferns and tightly woven vines. But soon enough this rich green world grew cool and foggy and the vegetation disappeared because the ground was covered by hardened volcanic ash and frozen lava.

"Listen here," Riley said, "I'll be clear, Engleburt dear. Let me say today what happened to Mt. Pelée."

"What do you mean," said Engleburt, a little scared by Riley's tone.

"I'll give you the facts I got from Max," said Riley.

They stopped walking and sat down on a bare tube of cold lava. Engleburt wasn't at all chilly—he was used to much colder weather in Antarctica. But still he didn't like even the slightest bit of cool.

"Let's go back down the mountain," he said. "I'd like to get into some warmer place."

"No," answered Riley, "we can't go yet—I don't want you to

forget what I'm going to say today.''

''Ok, but make it snappy,'' said Engleburt.

''In 1902 the mountain she blew—lava red hot spilled over the top killing people by the lot. Forty thousand died, broiled, boiled, or fried, while the blizzarding ashes fell on their lands below like a gray hot storm of snow. That's all I know.''

Engleburt just listened in awe to Riley's tale of volcanic eruption and destruction.

They sat silently for a long time.

The mountain seemed peaceful enough.

Engleburt could even hear birds singing and insects sawing. But when he looked toward the top of Mt. Pelée he realized that no vegetation grew on her brow—and he saw from her top a slight plume of white steam and smoke.

But Engleburt didn't say a word.

He wondered if he could settle on a mountain that had done such destruction.

He thought, though, that Mt. Pelée was just being natural—doing what volcanoes do. And after a little more thinking, he decided that it was alright to live there. He even thought it was—as Max promised it would be—a perfect place for his new settlement.

Mt. Pelée was isolated, rocky, full of caves—and on its higher slopes the weather was cool—for those penguins who might want a touch of the old home, while on its lower slopes it was very hot. And at its base were beaches of black volcanic sand and a wild stormy coastline of breaking waves. Yet there were coves and inlets of quiet waters.

Engleburt knew there were lots of fish in the waters around Martinique.

Finally, he said out loud.

''This is the place. Here I shall put my city.''

# Bruce Returns

ENGLEBURT began to make plans for his city. He checked smooth rocky hollows that would be good for nests. He furnished these nests with pebbles because penguins don't use twigs or grass—there being few fields and no trees in Antarctica. He made sure that the nests were in easy reach of the ocean. He made for himself two nests. One was a command nest in the highest reaches of the volcano. Here he could oversee the whole settlement. The winds ripped fiercely on this upper slope where hot volcanic steam belching from Mt. Pelée alternated with cold sea-borne foggy gales. Engleburt's other nest was down on the seashore, in the midst of the tropical heat. Here Engleburt hoped he could bring his wife—he remembered a few female penguins back in Antarctica who thought he was attractive. And here he would share with her the job of incubating their eggs.

Engleburt day-dreamed his family into existence. Three little penguin chicks, two girls and a boy. And a busy pair of parents, surrounded by friends, aunts, uncles, cousins—and the whole population of . . . but Engleburt hadn't thought of a name yet for his city.

What could it be?

Engleburt City? Penguin Haven? New Arctica?

No name seemed to fit.

Riley was getting impatient. She wanted to get back to the southern part of Martinique.

"Don't waste your time in this clime," she clucked. "I want to go down below." She didn't know what Engleburt was thinking. She didn't know that he was inventing inside his bird brain all the intricacies of a great settlement, a new country, an entire society.

"Why don't you go back alone?" Engleburt said. "I want to stay up here and think."

Riley knew her friend was strange.

He didn't like to play all the time like other young birds. He was a thinker, a planner, a leader.

Just then, above them, disappearing and reappearing in the quick moving low scudding clouds a small but brave pigeon circled and called.

"Hey, Riley! Hey, Engy!"

Engleburt and Riley looked up.

"I'm back! I made it through! I delivered the message!"

It was Bruce. He had flown all the way to Antarctica. He told the other penguins about Engleburt's adventures. He emphasized that Engleburt had found a good place in the sun for those penguins who wanted warmth to settle in.

Bruce was a fine ambassador of Engleburt's ideas. Bruce was excited by the prospect of having a whole bunch of new penguin friends.

He circled down and settled next to Riley and Engleburt.

He began to preen his feathers.

And he told them all about his flight and his meeting with the penguins of Antarctica.

Even Riley gave up the idea of heading back to the southern end of Martinique. She wanted to hear all about Bruce's mission.

He told them, sparing no details.

His final words were, "Yes, they're coming. A lot of penguins want to settle here in Martinique."

"And, I have some news of a private kind for you, Engy."

"What is it?"

"Riley, my bride, has inside her our first two eggs."

"Really," said Engleburt, "I'm so excited and pleased. Will you settle here with us?"

"When my eggs arrive," said Riley, "they could never survive up here, my dear."

"Don't be offended," Bruce added. "But Max has already made plans for us down at Club Med."

"That's ok," Engleburt answered. "I know we'll always be good friends. And maybe my chicks can play with yours."

"I hope so," Riley said. "But now we must be going—I feel my eggs growing. I can't stand and play, I've got to find the right place to lay my eggs today."

"Today!" shouted Bruce.

"Today, today, that's what I say," Riley repeated in a musical voice.

So up in the air mounted Bruce and Riley. They circled Engleburt three times, dipping their wings in happy salute, before they headed off to the south.

Engleburt was alone. He imagined all the great times to come. He saw in his mind's eye a vast city of nests, the crowding plumages of penguins, the flocks dancing to and fro over the black volcanic sands. In his mind's ear he heard the squeaking of thousands of penguin voices. He envisaged a great metropolis of penguins.

Exactly twenty-nine days later, penguins began to arrive in Martinique.

# Naming the City

A GREAT flock?

No, just seven hardy adventurous birds.

Engleburt could hardly hide his disappointment. But he was determined, as were the others.

Who were these pioneer penguins? There were Ethyl and Elizabeth, twin birds of great courage and imagination. By twins we mean that these penguins were hatched at the same time and grew up in the same nest. They did not come from the same egg. And then there was Andy, a playmate of Engleburt in the old days, and surely his best friend.

"Hi, Andy," Engleburt squeaked when he saw Andy. Engleburt was really glad that his good friend had decided to make the trip north to the sun.

"Glad to be here, Engy," Andy squeaked back very enthusiastically. "You sure seem to have things under control."

Those two soon went off for a swim together where they could share accounts of their mutual adventures during the months of their separation.

The other four of the seven arrivals were the Blackfooted penguins, Arthur, Carl, Ralph, and Morris. These young birds were about Engleburt's age, but considerably taller. They also talked a lot, as Blackfooted penguins are wont to do. When they got talking together excitedly, the Blackfooted cousins brayed like donkeys. Engleburt was an Adélie penguin with a gentler voice. These two species are closely related but even so the Blackfooted cousins didn't know Engleburt very well. They came north out of a passion for doing unusual things together. They knew of Engleburt's plans long before he set out on his great adventure—but, like so many others in Antarctica, the Blackfooted cousins thought he had probably perished during his long and perilous journey.

The four cousins were great jokers.

As soon as they saw Engleburt, Carl cried out in his donkey-like voice:

"Hey, cousin Adélie, there was a bullfrog and his human friend inside this house. And the doorbell rang. The human said, 'Bullfrog, you go into the other room.' The frog did, but left the door slightly open so he could hear everything his human friend said. The human opened the door, and lo and behold, standing there was a very fat, unathletic frog. This fat frog said, 'I can jump six feet!' The human answered, 'Bull, frog.' At which point bullfrog heard his name and rushed in from the other room! The unathletic frog shouted, 'I can so jump six feet!' Bullfrog said, 'I can jump eight, so what's so special about you, huh?' "

At the end of this joke, all four of the Blackfooted penguins doubled up and roared with laughter. Their violent braying howls could be heard throughout the whole rain forests. Down the slopes some farmers thought that wild jackasses had gotten in some kind of trouble.

Engleburt just stood still. He figured out that his Blackfooted cousins had a sense of humor all their own. They told long un-funny jokes. And they didn't understand funny jokes told to them. But they were hard workers willing to put all of their muscular efforts into building the city.

The city had no name.

Engleburt worried about this.

How can a city have no name?

He gathered all seven penguins together.

"We must name our city," Engleburt told them.

His seven comrades stood still. No one made a single suggestion.

"Come on," he said. "Each of you think of a name. I'll think of one too. Then you will vote without me to pick the name of our city."

Andy piped up, "Why won't you vote with us?"

"Since I'm here and I made all the arrangements, it's not fair that I pick the name of the city too."

The penguins thought a long time.

Elizabeth had what she thought was a great name.

"Let's call our city New Antarctica," she said.

"Brrr!" cried Andy. "That place is too cold. I don't want to remember it at all."

Then one of the Blackfooted penguins, Ralph to be exact, made his suggestion.

"Let's call it 'Cow Hill.' "

All four Blackfooted cousins laughed and laughed and laughed.

"Cow Hill! Cow Hill! Cow Hill!" they chanted in unison. None of the penguins, Engleburt included, had ever seen a cow. None of them even knew what a cow was.

How then did Ralph know the word?

That is a great mystery.

Engleburt shuddered when he realized that his new city would be named "Cow Hill." He wondered why in the world he had suggested a vote. He learned that day about the power of democracy. And even though he hated the name "Cow Hill" he knew that he had to accept the will of the majority. And that meant doing what the four Blackfooted penguins decided. They were a majority.

So that's how the first penguin settlement in the tropics got to be called Cow Hill.

# Cows and Penguins

DURING THE next few days Engleburt sent out another pigeon to Antarctica for more females. You see there was a big shortage of females at Cow Hill.

While waiting the penguins in Martinique decided to go ahead and build their city.

They gathered many many little rocks for the nests. Sometimes they had to build small wooden foundations for the rock nests as well as canopies of large palm fronds. Both the foundations and the canopies were necessary because the north end of Martinique gets lots of rain.

On the wood structures holding up the canopies the penguins —under Engleburt's supervision—painted pictures of cows and penguins.

Each penguin got to paint his own house.

Engleburt painted his house in the following fashion.

There were four posts holding up Engleburt's canopy. On each post he painted a fine picture. One was a self-portrait. But, truly, he didn't have enough room to paint it very well. In fact, Engleburt was a bit discouraged by his attempt at portraiture so he left the second post bare. On the third post he painted one cow, the Cow Hill cow. He found out from Riley what cows and bulls look like. On the fourth post he painted three small figures—one bull, one cow, and one penguin. The penguin was Andy, and Engleburt was very pleased by the way it turned out.

Under the canopy Engleburt built himself a nest. And next to the nest he built a small stove so that he could cook shellfish and finfish. Engleburt had acquired from his human friends a taste for cooked food.

The Blackfooted penguins wanted to live together. So they built an especially large, commodious house with four great palm fronds as a canopy. In their house there was room for four nests. The house's wooden foundation rose five feet from the ground. They painted the wood pure white—using crushed clam shells mixed with penguin saliva as pigment. They ground the shells and mixed the paint with their beaks. Then over this base of white they painted a self-portrait: four proud Blackfooted penguins, wing to wing, their beaks open as if they were all shouting together.

Engleburt looked at this edifice and the ornate painting and thought that the Blackfooted cousins had painted themselves reciting their bullfrog joke.

Then all of the penguins got together to construct roads joining every individual nest to a center plaza. The plaza was a wide open space with a big canopy of twelve palm fronds in the center. This was their meeting hall. This meeting hall contained three benches made from fallen logs. All the penguins of Cow Hill could sit on these benches at one time.

The roads to the center plaza, and the center plaza itself, were made of clam shells pressed into the rich dark earth of Martinique. Engleburt and his companions gathered many thousands of clam shells in order to pave their roads and plaza. They were very proud of their hard work, which took them more than three months.

The penguins also got very fat during that time—because they had to eat all the clams whose shells comprised Cow Hill's roads.

During the last couple of weeks of building the male penguins were eagerly looking across the southern horizon expecting at any minute to see a flock of female penguins swimming towards them.

Each day they looked, and each day the horizon was empty.

But then one day they saw something moving at the very rim of the horizon. It looked like it was coasting across the water. Andy was saddened because he thought "Gee, only one female decided to come north."

As whatever it was came closer they noticed it wasn't a penguin at all, but a flying animal—a bird. It was Bruce who was returning from his second journey to Antarctica.

"Of course," Engleburt exclaimed, "a pigeon can fly faster than a penguin can swim!"

"Hi, Bruce," the Blackfooted cousins shouted in close harmony.

Bruce circled in for a perfect two-foot landing on what the penguins had named Clam Boulevard.

"How'd your trip go?" asked Engleburt.

"Quick, gimme some water," Bruce panted. "It's been a terribly difficult flight back—and I haven't had a drop to drink for two days."

Andy brought back two big mussel shells full of clean, fresh water.

Bruce drank them down in a couple of gulps.

"More!" he exclaimed.

As Andy went for more water, Bruce began to tell the story of his expedition to Antarctica.

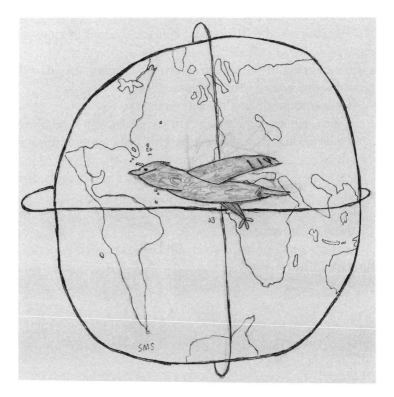

# Bruce's Expedition

"THE FLIGHT down was easy because I was flying with a wind pushing me south when I left. And when I got to Antarctica, many females—five or six—wanted to come to the tropics with me."

"Are they on their way?" asked the Blackfooted cousins.

"Sure are," said Bruce. "They'll be arriving in about two weeks time, I'd estimate."

"So what happened on your way back?" Engleburt asked.

"Well, it was this way," continued Bruce. "The first leg back—from Antarctica to the southern tip of South America was easy. But then the wind switched to a strong easterly blow. It pushed me right out to sea off the coast of Chile. I knew I had to get back to the Atlantic Ocean side of South America. But I just couldn't make any headway."

Here Bruce paused.

Andy came up to him and asked in his kindest voice: "Do you want more to drink? Or how about some fresh pine nuts to eat? Or maybe you'd like some shellfish—because we may be doing some more paving in village square."

Bruce nodded his head.

"Yes, something nourishing to eat would be good. I forgot all about eating.''

The Blackfooted penguins laughed.

''Do you want to hear our bullfrog joke?'' they asked.

Engleburt, Andy, and the twins groaned.

''Not again!'' Elizabeth screamed.

Then a silence settled over the group of penguins crowding around the brave pigeon. It was late in the day. The sun was low over the western sea. Andy brought some delicious oysters to Bruce, and a mussel shell full of cool water.

''Tell us more about what happened to you,'' Engleburt instructed.

''So there I was,'' Bruce continued, ''blown off course, in the middle of a wild and empty sea. Thirsty, hungry, scared, and exhausted.''

''It would have been a good time for Buster to show up,'' said Engleburt.

''Buster?'' asked Ethyl, the other twin, ''who's Buster?''

''Oh,'' said Engleburt, not wanting to interrupt Bruce's story with a story of his own, ''just a friend of mine.''

''So what did you do?'' asked Andy.

''I decided not to fight the gale,'' Bruce replied. ''I remember Max told me once—'When you're in trouble, fighting a force much stronger than you are, just go with the flow.' So that's exactly what I did. I relaxed, even closed my eyes, and just spread my wings and waited to see where the wind would carry me. At first there was nothing but ocean below me. Then, suddenly, I saw some islands underneath me. One of them was called Makemo, another Tahiti. I wanted to land and eat and drink, but the winds wouldn't let me descend. Then I passed over Society Island, and next there was Palmer Island. Finally I was pushed by the biggest wind imaginable over New Caledonia. It must have been a typhoon forming because the rain was terrible, the waves monstrous, the wind indescribable. But at least I got enough to drink.''

''What an adventure!'' cried Andy.

''Oh, it's not over yet,'' said Bruce.

"Then a northerly wind took hold of me and pushed me up to Namomuto Island. Then I was seized by a strong southeasterly wind and pushed to Japan. At last I had a chance to rest and meet other pigeons."

"Do you speak Japanese," asked the Blackfooted cousins.

"No," Bruce answered, "but the pigeons in Japan speak not only Japanese but International Pigeon—like we do here in Martinique. So I could converse with them very easily."

Bruce took a few gulps of oyster.

"Mmmmm," he sighed, "that's real good."

Then after still another mussel shell full of water, he went on with his story.

"In Japan I got real rested. But I also grew worried that I would be so far off schedule that you guys back here would panic. So I bid my Japanese friends goodbye and took off. Another wind caught me. It brought me to Yinchuan in China. There I couldn't land because there was a dust storm—so I just stayed with the wind which turned northerly and blew me right into India. And what a time I had there!"

Just as Bruce mentioned the word India, they all caught a whiff of the most delicious spicy aroma. After all, Martinique is in the West Indies—and a touch of the Orient is present there. Not to mention many people from India itself, as well as from Africa—and the descendants of the Carib peoples who populated the islands before any of the settlers from overseas arrived.

"What did you do in India?" Ralph asked.

"First I just drank lots of water and rested. But it's hard to rest in India with all the bustle. I saw such things! A snake charmer who played a clarinet and made the cobra dance."

Andy got very excited when he heard about the snake charmer. Andy was a heptologist—a scientist who studies the behavior of snakes. Andy was a very unusual penguin—he loved snakes, while most birds fear and detest them.

"It's cruel to 'charm' a snake," Andy said. "Do you know how they do it?"

The penguins crowded around Andy.

"Tell us," demanded Elizabeth and Ethyl. "Yes, yes, yes," chanted the Blackfooted cousins.

"The 'charmer' de-fangs the snakes—that means he pulls out the poor snake's teeth. And along with the teeth come the cobra's poison sacs, pulled right straight out of the miserable reptile's head. When the 'charmer' opens his basket, the only reason the snake comes up and wiggles his head back and forth is because he's hurting. It takes about six months for a snake to get over his agony. And then guess what happens?"

"What," Engleburt asked.

"The old 'charmer' gets a new snake."

The penguins were really upset by what they heard. None of them appreciated cruelty to animals.

"The name of the clarinet the 'charmer' plays is 'shenai'— and it really hasn't any affect on the cobra. It just looks as if the cobra is dancing to the music."

Bruce was quiet for a minute. He was glad to have the new information. But he was upset that Andy had ruined the tone of the gathering. How could Bruce go on with what else happened to him in India?

Bruce thought.

And thought.

Finally, he decided to go ahead with his story anyway.

"I appreciate what you've told us, Andy," Bruce said. "But I have to say that I had a terrific time in India, and at the time I even enjoyed the snake charmer. But now that I know the whole story I don't think I could enjoy that kind of show again. But what I also did see in India were elephants. I mean real, gigantic, bellowing—"

Andy couldn't restrain himself.

"Elephants walk on their tiptoes, even though they are so big," he said. "Their feet look as if they are walking flatfooted, but their bone structure is such that they really are walking on their toes."

"That's hard to believe," the Blackfooted cousins said in unison.

86

"They are beautiful animals," Bruce went on. "And I met a little boy who is an elephant trainer—they call him a 'mahut.' He was about ten years old. Everyday he had to take three elephants down to the river for their bath. A big old female, she was very handsome, a slightly smaller male who sometimes got a little grumpy, and a tiny baby. Nissar—that's the 'mahut's' name—told me that the big elephants were not the parents of the baby. The baby was an orphan that Nissar's employer got cheap after some really bad people had killed his mother for her ivory. The father had run away with the rest of the wild herd and the little baby was left to fend for itself."

Elizabeth wanted to know how Bruce got involved in all this.

Bruce said that he simply had gone to the bank of the Godavari River for a bath and a drink—and all of these things happened right there. The snake charmer, Nissar and his three elephants, and many other adventures that Bruce didn't have time to tell the penguins about at the moment. "I stayed in India for two whole weeks—I just couldn't bear to leave. I liked the people so much —and there are so many different kinds of birds, including peacocks—the fanciest member of the pigeon family."

Arthur, a penguin who hardly ever said anything by himself, piped up.

"I could tell you a thing or two about peacocks!"

Everyone looked at Arthur.

But Arthur was not going to say another word.

After a short pause during which the conference of birds looked out at the deep blue sea and the frothy whitecaps, Bruce went on.

"Then I was blown across the Indian Ocean directly into Kenya where I saw the Kikuyu people dancing. Then I got blown up into Niger and from there a big northerly gale swept me across the Sahara and the Mediterranean Sea into France. I had another stopover in France to get something to eat and drink. But by now I was very anxious to get back to you. So I took off and relaxed into the wind which carried me to the Cape Verde Islands. The trade winds carried me across the Atlantic to northern Brazil. And then, suddenly, the wind stopped and I had to work my way up the Atlantic and into the Caribbean. Finally I arrived back home. So here I am!''

All the penguins and all the pigeons who had assembled to hear Bruce's expedition cheered and squealed and clapped and clucked.

What a story!

What a bird!

# Mt. Pelée Blows Its Top

THEY WOULD have liked to hear more from Bruce. But there was lots of work to get done in Cow Hill. As they began pecking and pushing away twigs, rocks, and small debris in order to form the central area of the town, Engleburt thought he heard a deep rumble from up on Mt. Pelée. But he didn't stop working—he was too busy. He ignored the volcano's signal.

But he noticed that this northern end of the island was uninhabited—not only were there no people, which really was an advantage to the pioneers of Cow Hill, but there were relatively few representatives of the animal kingdom. And near the top of the formidable mountain all vegetation ceased. Up there was only gray volcanic rock. Engleburt actually thought this was an advantage—because from the rocky summit the penguin community could obtain raw materials for its nests.

Also looking up there reminded the penguins of their home in Antarctica where in the southern summer some of the gray rocks of the continent were exposed. In other places of Antarctica, the ice is a mile deep—so of course it never melts even in summer.

The other penguins heard the rumbling from the mountain, too. They looked at Engleburt, their leader.

"Nothing to worry about," he said.

But Bruce and a few other pigeons, crows, and even flamingos who were in the area began to speak noisily to each other. And the penguins noticed that the sparse settlements of fishermen were packing to leave. They were loading everything they could into their small motorboats and sailing vessels. Most of these sailboats had two sails, a small one in front and a bigger one over the middle.

These boats were so full of belongings, chickens, even goats and small cows, that they sank almost deep enough for the ocean to swamp them.

''People're clearing out,'' said Bruce. ''I don't think things are going to work out for Cow Hill.''

Deep in his heart, Engleburt had fears too. But he didn't know how to balance them against his commitment to building the new city for the penguins.

Engleburt reasoned to himself.

If I tell everyone to leave and there is no eruption, we will have wasted a lot of time. And maybe even some wild animals or people will come and ruin Cow Hill—because none of us will be here to guard it, defend it, or even let anyone know that this is a city of penguins.

But if we keep working and there is a terrible eruption, then there is a danger that my penguins will be burned, boiled in steam, smothered in ashes, buried in lava—and turned into rock. All that will be left will be lumps of former penguins, containing our bones encased in domes of lava.

While Engleburt was thinking so deeply, the other penguins noticed from the very top of Mt. Pelée plumes of steam and occasional puffs of white smoke.

It looked very beautiful.

Even peaceful.

The only real hint of big trouble was the almost continuous grumbling from way down in the guts of the mountain. And now, from time to time, a slight tremor, making all of Cow Hill rock up and down—as if it were built on a great big floating island rising and falling in a rolling sea.

Then at about noon of the second day of all this motion and steaming and puffing, Mt. Pelée gave the first real indication of what it had in store for Martinique. It gave out a big burp of ashes—huge, gray clouds. And showers of hardened lava rained down like hail.

The penguins took shelter in their small nests. They huddled against this strange blizzard of lava and ash. Soon the ash storm grew so intense that their houses started to collapse. They fled to the big main central structure with its solid roof of palm thatch and supporting columns of rocks.

Elizabeth, who was the youngest and smallest of the birds, cried out, "I'm scared! I know what to do when it snows—but what can I do now?"

Penguins are used to blizzards of snow, where the biting wind drives fiery points of snow up against their coats of feathers. Penguins are well equipped to defend against even the most terrible of blizzards.

But this was different.

And it was not only Elizabeth who was scared.

All of them—Andy, the Blackfooted cousins, Ethyl, and even Engleburt were terribly unsure of what was going to happen next.

They huddled together inside their main building. Through the darkening clouds of smoke and ash they saw flashes of purple lightning and even some fire flaring up from the summit of Mt. Pelée. Then Andy saw a dome of redness swell up from the very top of the mountain. This red dome grew like a giant bubble and then suddenly it burst and down the side of Mt. Pelée rushed a great river of molten lava.

Luckily, this river of red-hot rock wasn't aimed at Cow Hill. But the penguins all saw what Mt. Pelée had in store for their beloved new city.

Engleburt gave the signal.

"Now that the ash has stopped coming down," he said, "and the lava isn't here yet, we've got to make a run for it!"

He even smiled.

"I promised you all a good warm place to live—a tropical

paradise. Well, this is a little hotter than what I had in mind.''

"Can we take anything with us?" asked Ethyl.

"Better not," advised Andy. "We've got to clear out pronto."

So off they went, a straggly line of black and white birds rushing pell-mell down the side of a great erupting volcano. In their ears they heard crashing and roaring; above them they saw boiling clouds of ash; behind them the red fountains of lava spewed forth endlessly.

It was terrible but it was beautiful.

Engleburt turned around to take one farewell look at Cow Hill.

His head was facing up the mountain even as his feet carried him downhill.

Ooops! Engleburt's orange toes caught on the underside of a fallen log. He fell to his left side, wrenching his leg awfully. He heard a sharp crack from inside his left leg. The pain was sudden and intense. He let out a loud scream. He flashed on the time when he was just leaving Antarctica and he fell into a crevasse from which John and Veeny rescued him.

This time the Blackfooted cousins saw what happened. They rushed back as a team.

"Are you ok?" Arthur asked.

"I think my leg is broken," Engleburt said.

Luckily they were far enough down the mountain that the cousins could locate a couple of big palm fronds from which they fashioned a stretcher. Gently all four of them lifted Engleburt onto the stretcher. Then, moving more slowly than they wanted to, they continued their struggle down the mountain towards the seashore.

Engleburt was in pain, but he wasn't about to surrender his leadership. He knew that he would have to have his bone set and splinted. He feared he would not have enough strength or mobility to swim to safety.

Meanwhile, Andy, Elizabeth, and Ethyl reached the shore without realizing that Engleburt and the Blackfooted cousins were gone. Never looking back they plunged into the cool Caribbean, free at last from the threat of the rivers of lava rushing more insistently and approaching ever closer down the mountain.

When in his exultation Andy shouted above the frothy waves, "Hey, Engleburt, we may have lost Cow Hill, but we're alive!"

There was no answer.

"Engleburt! Engleburt!"

Then all three penguins stopped swimming. They surfaced and turned around to see a horrible sight.

The whole side of Mt. Pelée was ablaze in lava. The top of the mountain was exploding with black smoke and fire. And nowhere to be seen were the Blackfooted cousins or Engleburt.

Andy and the others swam in desperate circles, their eyes flooded with tears, their squeaks a terrible shrieking of grief, fear, and remorse. Such was the noise of the awful eruption of the giant mountain that they couldn't hear their own sounds.

But their grief was premature.

The Blackfooted cousins were very cool customers.

As soon as they realized that Mt. Pelée was really blowing its top, with lava streaming a mere fifty feet behind them, they dropped the stretcher and put Engleburt under their arms, carrying him like a stiff log. They ran with all their might to a cliff edge. Blackfoots are great runners, extremely sure-footed on ice, rocks, snow—any surface. And for all their braying, they were brave, loyal birds who respected and loved Engleburt. They rushed headlong for the edge of the cliff, swerving neither to the left nor right. As they jumped off the cliff, not knowing where they might land, one of them, Arthur, glanced backwards and saw the palm-frond stretcher burst into flame before it was engulfed by the lava.

There they were, in the air, flapping their wings—maybe the first penguins in history to fly, or almost.

Engleburt trusted the cousins with his life. He was gathering his whole mind to concentrate on keeping his broken leg straight.

The Blackfooted cousins saw the lava reach the edge of the cliff and pour over in a great molten rock waterfall plunging down on their heads.

Still they didn't lose their composure.

They swerved as one sharply to the left.

So the lava streamed past them, and as it did Engleburt smelled the pungent odor of burning feathers. Luckily, it was just their tail feathers that had been singed. Just as he saw the lava strike the water turning thousands and thousands of gallons of sea water into steam even as the molten stuff froze into black rock, he felt the Caribbean Sea come up around him. It was cool water, not boiling.

They were in the ocean. They were alive.

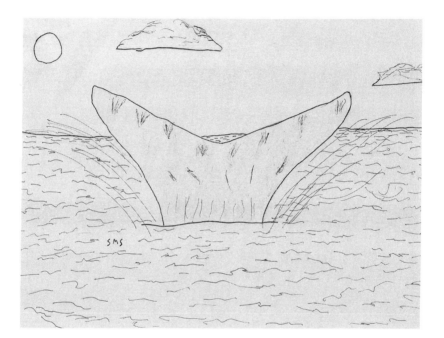

# Meeting an Old Friend

THEY WERE alive, but little else.

Cow Hill was destroyed by lava.

Mt. Pelée's huge plume of volcanic dust made noon look like dusk.

The penguins had to keep under water as much as possible to protect their feathers from falling dust— and worse, hot coals of chunky lava. As each of these coals the size of baseballs hit the water the ocean emitted a small puff of steam and the red hot lava instantly turned to black rock. This rock, called pumice, is very light, almost like cork—some pieces of pumice actually float, at least for a little while until their tiny holes fill with water and then they sink like small ships awash in a stormy sea.

Engleburt couldn't swim very well. But he was lucky.

If his wing had been broken, or his feathers severely burned, he wouldn't have been able to swim at all.

The Blackfooted cousins took very good care of him.

They surrounded him.

They sang encouraging songs to him, such as:

> Engy, Engy,
> Brave little pengy

> You can win
> You can swim
> You can make it through the day!

As they sang to him, the cousins looked around trying to find their comrades.

At the same time, Andy—who was a born leader—gathered Ethyl and Elizabeth.

"Come on, you two," Andy exhorted, "let's stay together. I'm sure Engleburt is ok. We'll find him somewhere."

But the female penguins were anxious. Not only about Engleburt but about Arthur and Ralph, Morris and Carl, the Blackfooted cousins. As a matter of fact, Ethyl had a crush on Ralph. She was plenty worried about him.

Elizabeth knew this.

She swam up close to Ethyl.

"Don't worry, dear," Liz said, "Ralph and the others are very inventive—and what's more, they always stick together—one helping the other, and that will make it easier for them to get through this."

"But what if they were caught under the lava?"

Ethyl imagined the most awful things.

"Or crushed by mountains of heavy ash?"

Just as she was thinking the worst, she thought she saw to her left a penguin's beak and shining eyes. And she thought she heard the excited stacatto braying peculiar to the Blackfooted species.

"Look over there!" Ethyl shouted.

Elizabeth and Andy immediately got very excited.

They jumped up into the air as far as they could.

They strained their eyes.

They focussed their ears.

And they heard a sound of familiar voices singing:

> Engy, Engy
> Brave little pengy
> Over here,

Very near,
We'll find friends, have no fear!

Soon the small troupe of penguins was reunited. They swam in formation around each other. Engleburt was so happy that everyone was alive and well that he forgot all about his broken leg.

But Arthur didn't forget.

"Engleburt hurt his leg," the quietest penguin said.

Andy asked to see it.

Engleburt was lifted partly out of the water by Ralph and Morris. Very gently Andy examined the broken leg.

"I'm not a doctor," he said, "but this seems like a simple fracture." That means that no bone is protruding through the skin.

"What we need is a splint," Elizabeth said.

"Where can we find one out here?" asked Ethyl.

None of the penguins were disturbed about being in the ocean—they could stay in the sea for weeks without any discomfort, especially an ocean as warm as the Caribbean. But Engleburt's broken leg was another matter. That had to be dealt with fast.

Then Ralph had a good idea.

"What about driftwood?" he asked.

"Yes," Andy answered excitedly, "and the eruption will have thrown lots of trees into the sea. There'll be plenty of material to make a splint from."

"Along with tons of palm fronds," said Ethyl. "That's what we can use to tie the splint on with."

Carl and Morris were assigned the task of staying with Engleburt helping him stay afloat but not letting him move his broken leg.

The other penguins scattered in all directions.

It didn't take them long to find the proper stuff to make a splint and to tie it on real tight.

But as soon as Engleburt was outfitted with his new splint, he began to worry.

"What are we going to do? Where are we going to go? I didn't bring you all up here just to watch a giant fireworks show.''

And that is exactly what Mt. Pelée was providing.

Giant plumes of fire and sparks were shooting out from its summit. Rivers of yellow and red molton lava were streaming down its flanks. And over the top a great cloud of ash was illuminated from within and below by the deep red of the volcano's fires, while purple flashes and bolts of lightning streamed out from the depths of this great boiling cloud.

If it weren't so destructive, if Cow Hill hadn't been crushed and burned by all that volcanic force, if thousands of rain forest animals weren't dead or dislocated, and millions of ferns and trees turned to charcoal, it would have been easier to enjoy the magnificant beauty of Mt. Pelée in eruption.

Still, it was nature's way.

The wisest penguins felt that.

All around them in the sea bobbed debris. Trees, bushes, logs, and lots of mud. Big clumps of earth, as if ripped up whole from the mountainside. And, sadly, one small piece of a human boat. When the penguins looked back up the side of Mt. Pelée to the place where Cow Hill used to be, they saw one scorched still smoking log from their beloved city. Only it was left to remind them of their courageous enterprise.

For two days the penguins swam away from Martinique and the exploding mountain. They ate what they could find—small fish and some mussels and barnacles attached to driftwood. Always the red glow and smoky plume of Mt. Pelée reminded them of where they had come from.

At around dusk on the third day they spotted a small island, treeless, awash in the ocean. It wasn't much, and they knew they wouldn't want to establish their new city there—but they thought it wouldn't be too bad an idea to rest there overnight.

So they swam over to the island and climbed up on it.

This was no easy task.

The island was so small and so wet that its beach was slippery. Everytime they got part of the way up, they slid back down. Engleburt didn't even try to go up.

"My friends," he said, "you rest for the night, I'll float out here, duck-fashion."

Usually, the penguins would want to do everything in an ensemble. But actually the others were more tired than Engleburt. After all, the Blackfooted cousins had carried Engleburt most of the way—with some help from each of the other penguins. Yes, they were very tired. As soon as each of them found a place on the tiny island, she or he fell fast and deep asleep.

The next morning dawned bright and clear. Mt. Pelée was nowhere in sight. This surprised Andy whose last memory of the night before was the glowing mountain.

Then Andy made a terrible discovery.

The island they were sleeping on was moving.

It was cruising through the ocean at a good fast clip.

"Hey, hey!" Andy shouted, "wake up! Ethyl, Arthur, Ralph, everybody! Wake up!"

The others, still bleary-eyed and full of dreams only partly forgotten, yanked themselves out of sleep.

Elizabeth was the first to say it.

"This is no island. This is a whale!"

And Arthur was the first to notice that Engleburt was gone.

"It's clear what happened," Andy said. "The whale started moving in the middle of the night while we were sleeping and Engleburt just stayed where he was."

"Where's that?" asked Elizabeth.

The Blackfooted cousins answered in harmony.

"Who knows? Who knows?"

Then their "island" stopped moving. And the penguins heard a deep grumbly thunderous voice.

"Hey, what's the racket up there?"

Andy jumped off the whale's back and swam up to one of his huge eyes.

"Let me explain—" he began.

But he didn't have time to get another word out.

"A penguin!" roared the whale in a voice so loud the whole

101

ocean shook. "A penguin!"

"Seven penguins," corrected Andy. "And there should be eight."

"The only penguin I know in these waters," the whale declared, "is my good old friend Engleburt."

Now it was the time for the penguins to be surprised.

"Engleburt!" shouted Andy. "You know Engleburt?"

"Know him?" Buster replied. "I dropped him off here. He and I traveled together all the way from Antarctica."

The penguins were stunned and happy.

"I'm just coming back from my big whale conference in the Bahamas." Then Buster noticed something.

"Where is Engleburt, that little rascal?"

"Well," answered Arthur, "when the volcano erupted—"

"What?" interrupted Buster. "Mt. Pelée has erupted?"

The penguins told Buster the whole story. They got up to the part where all the penguins found the small island to rest on. An island, it turns out, that was Buster himself. When they finished, Buster turned around and started swimming straight back the way he came.

"Wait for us!!" shouted the penguins.

And soon a small composite school of a blue whale and seven penguins streamed back towards Martinique.

Whales are equipped with spectacular sonar. It didn't take Buster long to locate Engleburt.

Engleburt, the night before, fell asleep on the sea next to the little island. He was desperately tired because of his great and perilous escape from Mt. Pelée. His leg had been bothering him, but not so much as to prevent him from falling into the deepest kind of mending sleep. He never heard the "island" swim away. When Engleburt woke up late the next morning, the "island" was gone.

He didn't know how to explain it. He thought he had drifted away during the night. He didn't know how he could get in touch with his penguin friends. But he wasn't scared for his life—at least not that much. He could keep afloat for days. He felt he could even dive down and catch a fish or two. And he knew Andy and the others would soon be searching for him. He was looking forward to being reunited with them.

So Engleburt decided that the best thing to do was to sit still and wait.

But when, at about noon, he saw a huge whale rushing towards him he was very surprised and more than a little frightened.

He controlled his fright with the fond wish that the great whale was his old friend Buster. "Then I'd be in great shape," he said to himself.

So you can imagine the joy in his heart when the whale got up close and called out, "Engleburt! Engleburt! It's Buster!!"

Broken leg and all, Engleburt flapped his wings and managed to rise a few inches off the water's surface. And then he all but flew to Buster's side. Engleburt didn't really fly, of course, but it looked that way—so fast did he propel himself toward his friend.

For his part, Buster leaped and breached and spouted and squeaked.

He was very happy too.

It was quite a show those two animals put on.

All around them gathered birds and dolphins and even some sharks and tuna and seagulls and herons—hundreds of birds of the sea and fishes. It was a great celebration they had that day in the Caribbean.

Engleburt forgot all about his leg.

Buster was laughing for hours on end.

Later that night, when things had quieted down, Engleburt told Buster all about what had happened since they parted. Buster told Engleburt all about the great conference of whales in the Bahamas. How the blues, humpbacks, sperms, grays, belugas, dolphins and even killer whales had come together. They discussed many things, especially the relationship between the whale species and the human species. And when they were finished confabbing, they threw a big party for themselves.

Engleburt said, "I'm really glad all the different kinds of whales can come together to talk about your common problems.''

''But let's deal with your problem,'' Buster offered.

''I wish you could help,'' Engleburt said, ''but how can you? You can't put Mt. Pelée back together again.''

''No,'' Buster replied, ''but I can steer you to another island—one with no volcano, no humans, but plenty of pebbly rocks and hills and caves. There's even a small glacier on the top of a small mountain.''

''No thanks,'' said Engleburt. ''I don't need any ice.''

''But what about some of your friends who may be homesick,'' Buster asked.

Engleburt knew his whale friend was right.

''I appreciate your suggestion,'' he told Buster. ''How far is this island of yours?''

''It's on the fringes of the Bahamas.''

''Are you sure we won't be disturbed?''

''No one can promise anything these days,'' Buster said. ''But I can be pretty sure you will be left alone. I don't think the humans even know this island exists.''

As Engleburt and Buster were talking, the other penguins had gathered around.

Ralph spoke up.

''It sounds great to me.''

And Ethyl chipped in, ''I want to climb up to the glacier.''

So without even voting, Engleburt knew that his little colony was going to try again on the island Buster would take them to.

# Buster's Island

BUSTER WAS more than glad to help Engleburt and his friends find a new place to live.

Buster knew all the islands in that part of the world. "During the days of whale hunters, we whales had to find nooks and crannies to hide in. It's not so easy to hide, you know, when you weigh 80 tons and are 100 feet long. My father, his name was Bump because he had a huge bump on his head where he got hit by a harpoon. The blubber just piled up over the wound."

The penguins all crowded around Buster eager to hear about his father, Bump.

"Well, my father got away from that harpoon, but he swore he'd never be in danger again. From that day on he began to search for safe havens."

"How many did he find?" asked Morris.

"Dozens," said Buster. "There were secret coves, and underground caves—and, as I said, islands scattered across the seven seas undiscovered by humans."

"That's hard to believe," argued Andy. Andy was the scholar among the penguins—he knew about animals and humans and even the workings of the tides and the weather. "I just can't believe that people haven't found every single island in the oceans.''

"You'll see," said Buster. "I'm going to take you to an island that no human being has ever discovered."

Engleburt couldn't wait.

During the couple of days when the penguins frolicked with Buster, Engleburt's leg grew stronger and stronger. He was looking forward to the day when the splint could be removed. The very fact that he was with his dear friend Buster again cheered him up immensely, and helped his healing. It also made him forget all the hard times at Cow Hill. In fact, the terrible eruption of Mt. Pelée became a fun memory, an adventure—a great story to be saved for his children and grandchildren. Maybe even his great-grandchildren.

Buster bellowed to the penguins, "Come on, follow me, I want to take you to my island."

Soon a regular parade formed on the Caribbean. It was mid-morning of the sixth day after the eruption that they all set in a line. Buster led the way, ploughing the waves with his immense body. Next came Engleburt, surrounded by the Blackfooted cousins who nudged Engy along. Then there was Ethyl and Elizabeth, swimming side by side, humming a happy tune. Andy brought up the rear—making sure all was proceeding according to plan.

And, lo and behold, who should show up overhead but a bunch of happy pigeons—Bruce and Riley and their four little babies: Riley's eggs had hatched and the pigeons had just learned to fly. With their bright flight feathers flapping, the young pigeons joyfully tasted the wind.

Buster was in no hurry.

He liked the warm Caribbean.

His conference was over—he had nowhere special to go.

Engleburt could not swim very fast, but no one minded.

Across the blue Caribbean they swam, moving steadily northward. They skirted Puerto Rico and headed for Haiti. They swam between the Dominican Republic and Cuba. Soon they were in the waters surrounding the Bahamas.

There are hundreds, yes, even thousands, of Bahamas. Only a few have human inhabitants.

Buster took his fleet far to the north.

When he got to the place he was looking for he blew three great blasts of water from his spout-hole.

In front of him was a rocky island, with two high hills, and not too much vegetation.

If the penguins had been birds like sparrows or robins or even parrots or birds of paradise, this rocky pile of rocks wouldn't look very attractive. Andy could understand how humans wouldn't care about Buster's island at all. He could also see the cove almost perfectly hidden from anyone looking in from the sea that had concealed Bump and his generation of whales, saving them from the savage hunters of whale blubber, meat, and oil.

The penguins were all excited by the island.

It was perfect.

It wasn't so big that they would feel lost.

There were plenty of rocks to build their special kind of penguin nests.

Buster promised Ethyl that indeed there was ice on the top of the highest hill.

And Engleburt was delighted with the warm tropical trade winds that blew in from the sea.

"What's the name of this island?" he asked Buster.

"Doesn't have any," the whale replied. "My father called it 'Bermuda,' but he was just joking."

None of the penguins except Andy knew what Bermuda was. But none of them bothered to ask Buster—they were too busy going ashore, pushing the pebbles and rocks around, exploring, climbing—checking the whole island out.

Riley and her small family were busy flying around investigating everything that looked interesting.

"This island's great, let's celebrate!" Riley rhymed.

And suddenly she produced from who knows where a styrofoam cup full of blueberry wine.

Bruce explained.

"Riley found the cup. And for weeks I've been storing up blueberries to feed the children. When the eruption happened I forgot all about my cache of blueberries. When I went back they had fermented and turned into this delicious wine!"

Engleburt gladly accepted the cup of wine.

He balanced it on his right wing.

He raised his head and beak toward Buster who was resting in the shallow water of the cove.

"I name this place 'Buster's Island,'" Engleburt declared. "And Buster's Island will be the new, and I hope permanent, home of all us tropical penguins. Here on Buster's Island we'll build our city and call it Penguina!"

The birds all cheered.

Buster blew another great stream of spout high into the air. Glistening in the sun it looked like fireworks.

"Hip, hip, hooray!"

"Cheers to Buster's Island!"

"Cheers to Penguina!"

Then carefully, even religiously, they passed the styrofoam cup from beak to beak, and each took a tiny ceremonial sip.

As they drank the ritual blueberry wine, Elizabeth saw on the horizon four, then five, then eight, then fourteen great gray hulks approaching them at a terrific clip. She wondered what these moving islands could be. She was a little afraid but because everyone else was so happy, she kept her fear to herself.

Ethyl saw the hulks too, but she knew what they were.

Whales.

Fourteen great giant blue whales.

Buster laughed at this surprise he'd arranged for Engleburt and his party. Because it was Buster who, using his high-pitched sonar voice, had summoned this convocation of behemoths. They converged on Buster's Island in order to put the final touch on the celebration.

Each blue whale had filled her or his spout-hole with different colored algae or seaweed or ground-up coral or brightly hued aquatic plants.

And then, on Buster's signal, they spouted together. A marvelous ensemble of bright colors. Fireworks at midday. Or, rather, spoutworks!

Maroon, lime, blue, orange, brown, gold, red, green, peach, purple, yellow, gray, silver, and even black!

Fourteen distinct colors, selected from the limitless palette of the oceans.

And as they spouted they squeaked out different songs with their high-pitched whale voices. These songs could not be heard in the air, but when Engleburt and the others swam below the surface they listened to the music of the whales reverberating through the depths of the Caribbean Sea.

Everywhere below there was music and everywhere above color.

The spouts were so strong that the penguins danced and swam in them, letting the colors stream down their black and white feathers, over their orange beaks and feet.

Riley and Bruce flew overhead through the multicolored display, carrying in their beaks small leaves and twigs for the new nest they were planning to share.

Then Engleburt, with Andy's help, swam out to Buster and gave him the sytrofoam cup full of blueberry wine.

Buster smiled with all his fifty thousand baleen strainers as Engleburt poured the last drops of the blue wine through.

Engleburt   Stories      by   Sam Macintosh-
                                  Schechner
    North To The Tropics        +
                              Richard Schechner